Cherishing Kitty

Cherishing Kitty

A Pride and Prejudice Variation

LEENIE BROWN

LEENIE B BOOKS

HALIFAX

Cover design by Leenie B Books. Images sourced from Deposit Photos and Period Images.

ISBN (print) 978-1-989410-55-4; (ebooks) 978-1-989410-53-0 (mobi), 978-1-989410-54-7 (epub)

Contents

Dear Reader,

Once upon a time...well, actually, a few years ago, I began a weekly writing exercise on my blog (leeniebrown.com) and called it Thursday's Three Hundred. What was supposed to be just a few minutes of practice – just three hundred words a week – quickly took on a life of its own and became something much grander.

Those writing exercises have now produced several published works, including the one you hold in your hands.

While some things about how I create these stories have evolved since that first writing exercise, the tradition of posting a portion of a story continues each Thursday. In fact, there is a story posting there now.

Prologue

Every dreadful step Lorcan Langley took down the corridor behind Matlock House's butler reverberated through him. His heart beat a steady and rapid rhythm while his lungs fought to fill themselves with air.

The interview which awaited him would not be an easy one, but not for the reason which everyone gathered in that small green drawing room would naturally expect. He had spent a restless night contemplating what needed to be done, and he had prepared himself as best he could to see that it was carried out

"Good morning, Mr. Langley." Mr. Bennet was the first to greet him when Lorcan entered the room. Mr. Darcy, as well as Lord and Lady Matlock, sat silently by, allowing the father of the lady he had compromised to begin the interview.

Langley pulled his eyes from the beautiful daughter seated next to her father and bowed his greeting.

"Please, be seated," Lord Matlock offered.

Langley considered refusing for what he had to say would not take long, but then, he thought better of it and sat. There was no reason to displease the gathered throng before he had to do so.

"I have heard your particulars from Lord and Lady Matlock," Mr. Bennet began. "You are well-established and would make a fine choice for that reason. However, I cannot say that I am pleased to have to consider you for the reason I must."

"I understand, sir. I acted inappropriately, and there is no excuse for my behaviour." He barely refrained from rubbing his sweaty hands on his breeches. Having been Lord Westonbury's friend for so many years had given him ample amount of practice with facing authority figures who were displeased, but all of those meetings with head-masters or his own father were child's play compared to facing the father of the lady whom he had been caught kissing.

He swallowed. He had not cried while being reprimanded since he was ten, but at present, he felt a tremendous urge to shed more than a few tears.

"I respect your willingness to take responsibility for your actions, young man," Mr. Bennet continued.

"To a point." Lorcan exhaled slowly as the words he had forced out settled on the others in the room. "What happened yesterday will not happen again. However..." He winced. The next part of what he had to say would be the hardest. "The incident was only witnessed by members of Miss Bennet's family; therefore, as long as none of her family share the story, there is no need to force a marriage where..." He closed his eyes so that he could not see Kitty's look of surprise. "There is no desire for one." He opened his eyes but kept them diverted from looking at Kitty by studying the floral pattern on the rug beneath his feet.

"On either side?" Mr. Darcy asked in surprise.

Langley lifted his eyes to the man. "Yes." And with that lie, he stood. "I have been called home; therefore, I will not be in town to cause any further unease to anyone."

"I trust all is well at home." Lady Matlock sounded skeptical.

"Yes. All is well. I am not leaving for an emergency." He was leaving because he could not be here and see Kitty, the lady who held his heart, being courted by other gentlemen.

"And what if there are rumors. We had several guests at Matlock House yesterday for Westonbury's wedding breakfast. Servants are known to carry tales."

"Not your servants, my lady." He held her fearfully intent gaze.

"I should hope that you are correct, but one never knows. From what I have been told the embrace which was witnessed was particularly passionate."

Oh, she was not wrong. It had indeed been passionate, and not just on his part. He could likely still feel Miss Bennet's fingers lacing through his hair and holding him to her as she pressed herself against him — if he were to allow himself the freedom to remember the interlude, that is.

He had not intended for the kiss he stole to become so ardent, but one touch of her lips to his had driven all rational thought from his mind. She was intoxicating in all the best ways. Unfortunately, just as many a foxed fellow does, he had, in his inebriated-by-desire state, stumbled and caught himself by placing his hand on the piano before which he and Kitty stood. That crash of keys had been the alarm which had brought his world tumbling down, in jagged pieces, around his ears and was why he was here now, staring down Lady Matlock.

"Such a tale might be too tempting to keep secret," she added.

"You know where to send for me if I am needed. I assure you, my lady, that I am not shirking my duty."

"Are you certain this is what you want?"

Langley turned away from Lady Matlock to find Mr. Bennet observing him with great interest and a hint of compassion. He allowed himself to glance at Kitty. Her cheeks were flushed, and her jaw was firmly set. She did not look at all pleased with how things had progressed this morning. However, he did not know why she should look so stricken. This was what she wanted. She had made it perfectly clear yesterday that she had no intention of marrying him. One would have to be excessively stupid to misconstrue "I am not marrying him" to mean anything other than the lady had no desire to be his wife.

He nodded as he turned back to her father. "It is." This lie did not fall any easier from his lips than any of the others had so far today.

"Well, then, Mr. Langley, if things can be kept quiet, I will absolve you of any duty to my daughter. However, if you change your mind..."

Langley clamped his teeth together tightly and gave a sharp nod of his head before looking at Miss Bennet one final time and leaving the room and any hope for a happy future behind him.

Chapter 1

How had it come to this?

Kitty Bennet surveyed her very lonely bedroom from what used to be the comfort of her window seat. This place of refuge was still filled with as many cushions as it had been before she had gone to town. There was no lack of comfort here for that reason.

There was still that secret pocket on the back of one of the pillows where she could hide letters, and the book where she pressed the flowers that she received from hopeful gentlemen was still hidden behind it. It was not that this seat lacked a feel of familiarity or of privacy.

It had all of those things. Though this window seat was, in every physical aspect, the same place where she had, as recently as two and a half months ago, sequestered herself away to dream about her future, since returning to Longbourn, it felt cold and barren.

She pulled the book of pressed flowers from its hiding spot and flipped through the pages looking at the meaningless symbols of admiration. With a sigh, she snapped it shut and pushed it away from her and toward the far end of the bench. There was nothing of real value in it. A few dreams. A multitude of wishes. The pleasant idea that someday the gentleman who gave her a flower for her book would be the one who would also claim her heart and offer his in return.

She pulled her feet up and wrapped her arms around her knees as she rested her head against the wall and closed her eyes. Sorrow wished to spill out of her, but she would not let it – at least, she would not until she climbed into bed. Then, knowing that no one would hear or see her, she would allow her heart to feel the cracks that scarred it. For now, she would strive to think of nothing – not of how all her sisters were married or soon would be, not of the soirees and possible matches which had been missed because she had been required to leave town before the end of the season, not of the dear friend she had left behind at Darcy House, and most especially, not of Mr. Langley. One tear sneaked out the corner of her eye, forcing her to brush it away.

"Miss Kitty?"

Opening her eyes, Kitty gave only a nod of acknowledgment to the maid who had entered since forming a reply of words seemed as if it would be far too much effort at present.

"Your mother has requested that you join her in the sitting room."

Kitty sighed and forced out the required words. "I will be down directly."

Then, she closed her eyes again – just for a moment. Morose thoughts must be pushed aside for now. She could entertain them for no more than these two heartbeats. Mama likely had callers since it was that time of day.

Rising from her place of repose and reflection, she crossed to the dressing table, took account of her hair and complexion, and, giving her cheeks a quick pinch, left her room.

~*~*~

"Oh, Mr. Bennet, is it not the best news?"

Kitty paused outside the sitting room. Was Papa once again not in his study? It was remarkable how often he seemed to be wherever her mother was. It had not been like this before she and her sisters had left for town, but, in the few weeks since Kitty had returned to Longbourn, she had found her father and mother not only in the same room but also having conversations and... she smiled as she spied it... holding hands. It was delightful to see such affection between her parents.

"I will not argue that it is a wonderful invitation, but do you not think it is too soon?" Her father's serious tone caused Kitty to pull back from entering the room as she was about to do.

"Oh, Thomas!"

Again, Kitty found herself smiling at the sweetness which seemed to flow between her parents now that all of their children were gone – well, all, save for her.

"She has been punished enough. I dare say she will not be kissing any other gentlemen."

"I should hope not!"

"Her heart is broken, Thomas."

Kitty rested a hand on her broken heart which had suddenly started to beat more rapidly. They were talking about her! And her mother had discovered her sorrow. Kitty had thought she had hidden it well enough, but apparently, she had not.

"She refused him," her father said.

Kitty swallowed the pain that those words brought. It was true. She had refused Mr. Langley, but not permanently. She had only meant it for a time. However, she had never been able to share that bit of information with him before he had rejected her. She supposed she should feel fortunate that she had discovered that his affection for her was less than hers was for him before she had made an utter fool of herself, but she was not.

"She is young, and you know how Lydia was always the one to lead the gentlemen around and decide who she and Kitty would favour with their attention. Kitty has not yet found her feet, and she will not find them here. Do you really wish for her to marry a captain in the militia? Her sisters have all done far better than that, and she is just as pretty as any one of them."

"I wish for her to find a gentleman who has both a fortune and who loves her." Her father sighed. "I had high hopes for young Langley from what I had been told, but it seems there is actually one gentleman in England who can resist the bewitching charms of your daughters. I truly had not thought it possible."

"Not all is over just yet." Her mother sounded a great deal more positive than either Kitty or her father were.

"You realize, of course, that your good news will see you left quite forlorn of any female companionship."

"I have my sister," Mrs. Bennet replied.

From her vantage point, Kitty could see her father kiss her mother's fingers.

"I have no greater wish than to see them all happily settled, Mr. Bennet."

"Even if that means they may be far from you?"

Her mother dabbed at her eyes. "Yes, even if they are far from me. I have always known that the best matches would not come from Meryton."

"But still it is not easy, is it, Mrs. Bennet? I find I am dreadfully lonely at times, and I am only their father."

"*Only? Only* their father?" Mrs. Bennet cried. "They could have no better father than you. There is no *only* about it." Her mother cast a look at the door. "What could be taking her so long?"

"I am certain I do not know." Her father kissed

her mother's fingers once again. "But I am not displeased to have a few more minutes with you all to myself."

Well, that was enough listening! Kitty smoothed her skirts and drew in a deep breath before entering the sitting room.

"There she is," her father said with a smile. Her mother attempted to pull her hand away from him, but he would not relinquish it. "You are to be sent away," he said to Kitty.

"Oh, Mr. Bennet! Do not tease her so!"

"I am not teasing. We are sending her away."

"That sounds far too harsh," Mrs. Bennet reprimanded. "What your father means is that you have been invited to stay with Jane before returning to town next Friday."

Returning to town? Kitty wished to inquire about that surprising bit of news, but her mother did not allow her a chance.

"Jane has never prepared a house for an extended absence, and, in her delicate condition, Mr. Bingley has asked if you would be willing to assist her."

"Unless, of course, you do not wish to help her." Her father's eyes were twinkling with mischief.

"Not want to help Jane? Well, I never heard of such a thing, I can assure you! One sister not helping another? It is not natural – at least, it is not when it is my girls."

"About returning to town?" Kitty inserted. That bit had still not been explained.

"Your mother and I agree that your punishment for your improper behaviour is over. We trust that you will refrain from throwing yourself at any gentlemen until such time as you have said your vows in front of a parson."

"I did not..." Kitty pressed her lips together at her father's glare. He had been excessively angry with her. She had not seen him so angry since Lydia had gone missing while they were at Darcy House. "I will not throw myself at any gentlemen," she promised.

"And you will not allow them to persuade you into impropriety either, will you?"

"No, Papa." She had no desire to do more than smile at a gentleman and accept a dance if asked. To do more, especially while in town, was dangerous. Gentlemen, just as Miss Darcy had feared, were duplicitous and only interested in a very limited number of things a lady could provide, and since Kitty had no fortune, the number of interesting things about her was even further reduced.

"Go on, my dear. Tell her the rest."

Mrs. Bennet, who had finally freed both of her hands, clapped them together. "You are going to Pemberley."

Kitty's brow furrowed. Pemberley was not in town.

"First, you will accompany Jane to town, and then, you will join Miss Darcy and accompany her to Pemberley. Town is just not tolerable during the summer, you see. All those who can leave town in quest of fresher air and open spaces. Why, even your aunt and uncle will leave town during the worst of the summer for a few weeks. You can return with them if you wish, or you can travel with Jane and Lydia when they return for the wedding."

The stream of information flowing in Kitty's direction stopped long enough for her mother to take a quick breath. Then, it continued as rapidly as it had before.

"Mr. Bingley is not giving up Netherfield until he has found something suitable elsewhere and most certainly not until after Lydia is married. We shall need the rooms for guests. We have space here, but I think that Lord and Lady Matlock would prefer the rooms at Netherfield, do you not agree? It would be an honour to have them here, but I must not think of myself. It is enough of an honour to have them be part of our family." She sighed. "An earl is a member of my family."

"And your daughter is a viscountess," Mr. Bennet reminded her, eliciting a further sigh. "You have done very well for yourself, my dear."

"Indeed, I have. So well, in fact, that it does not even matter to me that Charlotte will be mistress of Longbourn."

"We have just you, Kitty, of whom to dispose."

Kitty rolled her eyes at her father's taunt.

"But I do not wish to do so because it is required." The smile of a moment ago had been replaced by a stern expression.

"I promise I will not allow myself to be compromised." How many times was she going to have to assure her father that she was not the sort of girl who allowed just any fellow liberties? It had only been one fellow. One very special fellow, whom she had thought she was going to marry – eventually, as soon as her duty to her friend was complete.

Her father's head tipped as he silently scrutinized her. "Your mother and I love you."

Kitty blinked. Had he ever said such a thing so directly before? She did not think so. Love was assumed and demonstrated in various ways, and she had never in her life – not even once – felt unloved. However, she had also never heard her father say he loved her.

"I see I have shocked you." He chuckled. "We wish the best for you, just as we have and do for your sisters. Do not deny us that wish."

Tears were once again threatening, and on a shaky breath, she replied, "I will not," although she secretly feared she may have already done so, for she doubted if any gentleman could ever make her has happy as Mr. Langley had for those few short weeks in town.

"There will be another." Her father had risen and was now standing before her with his hands on her shoulders. "You are far too beautiful, charming, and caring for there not to be another gentleman out there who will fall deeply in love with you and endeavour to deserve you." He winked at her. "There will be another."

She was not certain he was correct, but she smiled as he patted her cheek.

"Your father is very wise," her mother added. "Hearts mend, but bags do not pack themselves. Off with you to make preparations. Jane expects you for dinner."

Today? She was leaving Longbourn today?

"You only need enough for a few days. The rest can be delivered later. Netherfield is only three miles away, you know. Go on. Mr. Bingley's carriage will be here to collect you at half four."

Kitty glanced at the clock on the mantle. Two hours! She only had two hours to prepare.

Her mother caught her hand when Kitty turned to leave. "I will miss you."

"And I, you," Kitty assured her before wrapping her in a quick embrace and then scampering away to do as she was told.

Chapter 2

"Stop scowling at me," Alfred Langley said to his cousin. "It was Father who decided you should accompany me. It was not my doing."

"Accompanying you would mean I was sitting in your carriage instead of my own," Lorcan Langley returned. "I am *escorting* you. And it was your mother not your father who insisted I must."

And he was none too happy about it. He had no desire to return to town and see Kitty driving through the park or dancing at a soiree with some fortunate dunderhead. A month and three days were not long enough for him to have forgotten her. He shook his head. A lifetime would not be long enough.

"You are only the transportation," Alfred assured him.

Lorcan snorted. "And leave you to your own

devices when I know your mother will be inquiring from *me* how you are getting on? I think not." His aunt was rather protective of her youngest son, which was why his uncle had come to the conclusion that Alfred travelling to town with Lorcan was a better option than Alfred travelling on his own.

"It is not as if I am going to immediately run the streets of London looking for a lark and land in Newgate. You should know me better than that, and I will have you know, this is not my first foray into town."

"None of that matters. Your mother tasked me with seeing that you were returned to her whole and undamaged — if you must be returned at all, that is." Lorcan chuckled at the way his cousin rolled his eyes. "You do have to marry someday."

"And to an heiress, if at all possible," Alfred said in a high-pitched tone. "And it would be lovely, *simply lovely* if she was a sweet girl," he continued in the same tone before giving a shake of his head and an exasperated huff. "I am twenty-six. I am not so old that I must have a wife or Mother will have no grandchildren. Look at Abraham. He was one hundred when Isaac was born. I have at least seventy-four years left before I need to worry."

"It is logic such as this that has made me your guardian."

"Guardian! I need no guardian. However, you can be my companion, though it is usually the other way around, is it not? Does not the older lady take on a younger companion? You might be too old for me." He straightened a sleeve while looking rather imperious. "I might have to sack you when we reach town in favour of a livelier and much younger gentleman to keep me company."

"You are not sacking me, and I am not that much older than you."

"Four years."

"Nearly four. I am not yet thirty, and you are just twenty-six."

Alfred shrugged. "You are still older and duller."

"I am not dull."

"You *were* not dull. However, you have *become* a positive bore. I do not know what happened when you were in town this season, but you have become disagreeable and grouchy. I dare say we should be taking you to Bath to stave off the gout before it sets in."

"Leave off," Lorcan snapped. He had no desire to discuss what had or, more precisely, had not happened in town.

Alfred's eyebrows rose. "Are you missing your friend Westonbury? Is that what has you in the doldrums."

"Yes." Although that was only part of it.

Lorcan had to admit he was jealous of his friend's good fortune, which now kept them apart. For, how could he visit Westonbury when Lady Westonbury would only remind him of her sister and the emptiness of his heart?

"Perhaps it is I who should have been entrusted with *your* care. I am certain I could find someone to take you on. I did help my brother." Alfred's chuckle was nearly menacing.

"I have no desire to be discovered in dishabille by any lady." Even if that lady was the one he hoped to persuade to marry him, as it had been for his elder cousin, Edgar. "Especially," he added by way of further caution, "if the young woman is to be followed in such a discovery by her father before she has a chance to slip away."

It had, supposedly, been an accident that Miss Crowther had stumbled upon the pond in which

Edgar had been swimming. However, the fact that Edgar's clothing had been moved from where he had left them near the pond to the limbs of a tree several feet away was not an innocent accident. Alfred enjoyed life with abandon at times, though he had not intended for his prank to end with his brother being forced to marry. Alfred, being quite young, at the time (Edgar was twelve years his senior) and having been a perfectly annoying youngster, had only wished to torment his brother.

"It has all worked out for the best," Alfred said by way of excuse.

"You are fortunate it did."

"I will grant you that. However, we all knew that Ed loved Ellen, and Ellen loved Ed. And I would further point out, that kissing a lady when only clad in a towel, whether or not you love her, is stupid – unless, of course, she is your wife already."

Alfred had a point there. Kissing a lady whom one loved but had not yet made one's wife was always a bit stupid. Lorcan knew that all too well. He would have done well to remember such wisdom before kissing Kitty, and, while part of him regretted having not refrained from kissing her, the other part of him, the part which refused to let him forget her, was happy he had not been wise. That part of his heart could only cherish the bitter-sweet memory of her lips on his and the softness of her form in his arms.

"You have no retort?"

Lorcan shook his head. "You are right. It is stupid."

His cousin's brow furrowed, and his head tipped to the left. "Did Westonbury steal a lady from you? Is that who he married?"

Lorcan shrugged and shook his head before nodding. "Westonbury did steal a lady from me, and she is now his wife. However, I am not angry with him any longer, nor did I know he loved her when I called on her."

Alfred whistled. "No wonder you are a dull grump. I suppose such disappointment cannot always be avoided with a friend such as Westonbury since he is both a viscount and a charming rascal. I would not wish for such a friend. It would make finding a wife much harder."

It did seem that way. However, it was not the viscount who had presented Lorcan with the dismal future which he now lived. That honour went to Lady Westonbury's sister.

"It is growing late," Alfred said when Lorcan did not reply to his comment about Westonbury. "Perhaps we should stop in Meryton and then continue to town tomorrow." Alfred's stomach rumbled. "As it is, we have to stop for the horses."

"That will not do. While we must stop for the horses, and you may get something to eat while we are at the inn, I wish to arrive in town tonight." He had no desire to stay in Meryton for it was far too close to Longbourn, and he had no wish to be reminded of the reason for his broken heart for any longer than was essential for refreshing both the horses and his cousin.

"But it will be dark before we get to town."

"Quite likely."

Again, his cousin studied him closely. "First, you grumble about having to return to town, and now, you seem anxious to get there. What are you not telling me?"

"Nothing. I am just tired of travelling."

"Which is an excellent reason to stop at the inn in Meryton."

"There would still be travelling to do in the morning. I prefer to have it all completed today. It is not that far from Meryton to town. We will push on today." He raised an eyebrow at his cousin and affected a look that often worked to silence Alfred. He just needed to get beyond Meryton without his heart putting itself on display for one and all to witness its tattered state.

Thankfully, the glare worked, and Alfred flopped back against the squabs while Lorcan turned his eyes to watch the countryside.

They were very close to Meryton, it would not be much further. Lorcan's eyes drank in the vistas Kitty must have seen many times. He had travelled this road often, but the scenery had never fascinated him as it did now since he knew that this was where she had grown up. Why he found it necessary to torture himself with thoughts of her when she would never be his, he was uncertain. It was as if Kitty Bennet had cast some unbreakable spell over him, and that dark magic drew him to her even when he knew she had rejected him.

A large home appeared in the frame of the window. Ah, that must be Netherfield. It was, indeed, just a stately as Kitty had described it to be. He blew out a breath. Three miles after that would be Longbourn. His heart quickened its pace, and Lorcan attempted to prepare himself for passing by her home.

However, not long after passing Netherfield, as dread and curiosity warred within him, the carriage lurched, sending him forward toward his cousin.

"You could have asked for a hug. You did not have to throw yourself at me," Alfred attempted to quip once the carriage had come to a halt at the side of the road. It rested at a strange angle, but, at least, it was still on the road and upright.

Lorcan pushed himself away from his cousin. "Your head is harder than I had thought," he attempted to jest in return as he rubbed his aching temple.

"Edgar always said it was." Alfred was also rubbing his head, only he rubbed his forehead. "I would say hard heads run in the family."

"Likely a gift from our fathers." Both his father and his uncle were men who were not easily swayed. If they had been, Lorcan would not be here now, sticking his head out the window and calling, "Is everyone well?" He would be safely tucked far away from Longbourn.

"Mostly," came the reply. "There will be a few

sore limbs, but no one lost their seats." Lorcan's coachman had climbed down from his box and was approaching the door. "A wheel has broken."

"Did you not inspect it for weaknesses before we set out?" Lorcan climbed out of the carriage.

"Yes, as always. We have travelled some rough stretches of road."

He could not deny the truth of that. Winter was not a friend of the roads, and the rain, of which there had been much lately, was even less friendly with the roads than the cold and snow of winter were.

"There is a house behind us. Likely not more than half a mile from here," his coachman suggested.

Netherfield.

"The wheel is not destroyed," his driver continued. "It is a minor crack if there can be such a thing. With a little patching, I am certain I can limp the carriage along to Meryton, but it would be easier and safer to do without passengers."

"Are you certain it is safe for you?" Lorcan knew from the intensity in his servant's eyes as he waited for his master's approval of his plan that the man feared a further break would not be a mere inconvenience as it was now. It would result in injury or worse.

"No, I am not, but I will ride postillion and will put one of the grooms on the other horse."

Lorcan rubbed the back of his neck while he studied Netherfield. He had no great desire to go there, but he also did not wish to walk to Meryton or remain on the road. "And what if no one is in residence?"

"There will be staff, sir. They will be able to help you find accommodations. Send a footman to Meryton if there is an issue, and I will hire a carriage to collect you."

"Very well," Lorcan agreed. There really was not much else to do.

"Ho! A carriage!" one of the grooms cried.

Lorcan turned to look toward Meryton. There indeed was a carriage coming toward them. He rubbed his sore head again and sent a prayer heavenward that the carriage was not Mr. Bennet's.

"Are you in need?" the coachman from the approaching carriage called.

"We have a broken wheel," the groom shouted back.

The carriage with four good wheels drew to a

stop, and Lorcan's groom joined one of the carriage's grooms in speaking to someone inside the carriage. Lorcan moved closer so that he could hear what was being said.

"We cannot carry our passengers. They will need a place to rest," his groom was saying.

"Of course, we can assist," came the reply from inside the carriage.

Then, to Lorcan's delighted surprise, Charles Bingley stepped out of the vehicle. Lorcan could manage spending a bit of time with Bingley – even if it did require him to also spend time with Kitty's eldest sister who was now Mrs. Bingley.

"Langley," Bingley cried. "It is very good to see you." Though the man wore a smile, he glanced nervously back at his carriage. "I believe we have room for – is it two passengers?"

"Yes, and a place for a groom."

Bingley nodded. "That is absolutely doable." He looked at the groom who had hailed his carriage. "See that Mr. Langley and –" He looked at Lorcan.

"Alfred Langley, my cousin," Lorcan supplied.

"See that both Mr. Langleys' things are transferred. We have several empty rooms just waiting to be occupied." Again, he cast a nervous look toward his carriage.

"We can stay in Meryton," Lorcan offered.

"Nonsense. I am sure we will get on just fine at Netherfield." He sounded confident, but there seemed to be hesitance in his expression.

"Are you certain?"

"Yes, yes. I am sure it will all work out as it should."

That seemed a strange thing to say.

"We were just visiting my wife's parents," Bingley continued.

"At Longbourn?"

"Where is Longbourn?" Alfred asked.

"About two miles ahead of us," Lorcan replied. "Forgive me, Alfred, this is Mr. Charles Bingley, friend of and, now, brother to Mr. Fitzwilliam Darcy."

"Ah, yes! You married Mrs. Darcy's sister," Alfred said.

"Indeed, I did marry one of her sisters."

"And Westonbury married another," Alfred added.

"And his brother is betrothed to another sister," Lorcan said.

"Indeed? Four sisters?"

Bingley shook his head and looked apologetically at Lorcan. "Five."

"Five?"

Did his cousin have to sound so shocked at that fact? And could they perhaps not speak of that fifth sister?

Bingley nodded.

"Is she married or betrothed?"

Bingley once again cast an apologetic look in Lorcan's direction. "No, not yet." He paused and then lowered his voice. "She does not even have a suitor at present."

She did not? How could that be? Kitty had been popular at all the soirees she had attended. He expected that the minute he had departed town, Banks would swoop in and snatch her up. He had seemed rather smitten with her. Not that Lorcan could blame him.

He followed Bingley to the carriage as his and Alfred's things were being moved.

"Jane, we have two more guests," he called to the occupants of the vehicle.

More guests?

"Do you already have guests? We can stay in Meryton," Lorcan offered again.

"We only have one guest for a fortnight before we return to town." He pulled the carriage door open. "My wife's sister."

Lorcan stumbled back a step. "We should stay in Meryton," he whispered.

"Are you well?" Alfred asked. "Did you hit your head harder than I thought?"

"Are you injured, Mr. Langley?" a sweet voice called out to him.

"Not overly so, Miss Bennet," he assured her. "My cousin and I merely knocked heads." It was good that she was concerned about him, was it not? No, he scolded himself, he must not hope.

"We must apologize for importuning you, Mrs. Bingley," he said as he entered the carriage. "Mrs. Bingley, Miss Bennet, this is my cousin, Mr. Alfred Langley. We were on our way to town when a wheel broke."

"You were returning to town?"

Was that a question or an accusation, for, to Lorcan, Kitty's tone sounded accusatory.

"Yes, my aunt does not trust my cousin to see to

his own health and well-being. Therefore, I am his escort."

"Companion," Alfred corrected with a smirk. "Mrs. Bingley, Miss Bennet, it is a pleasure to meet you. Would that the circumstances surrounding our meeting were better, but it is a pleasure none-the-less. And I would like to assure you that I am capable of seeing to myself quite well. It is just that when it comes to worrying, my mother is proficient."

Kitty giggled, and Lorcan wished to push his affable cousin, who was smiling far too charmingly at her, from the carriage – preferably, while it was moving.

Chapter 3

"Are you well?" Jane poked her head into Nether-field's music room.

Kitty, who was lying on a chaise in a pose she imagined one might fall in if one swooned, did not remove her eyes from staring at the ceiling. "I am."

She had been lying here like this since after she had made sure that her things were in her room as she wanted them. She had hoped this would be a good place to hide. And it had been until now.

"I am not entirely certain I believe that." Jane crossed the room. "I have not heard one song played since you entered this room thirty minutes ago." She pushed Kitty's legs over and sat on the end of the chaise.

"Did you see me come in here?" Kitty had thought she had sneaked in unawares.

"No, but a maid did."

Ah, that explained how her sister knew she was in the music room and for how long, for there had been a maid in here just finishing some dusting when Kitty entered.

"I thought it better for hiding if I did not play."

"You are hiding?" Jane asked in surprise.

Removing her arm from where it draped across her forehead, Kity shifted so she could look at Jane. "Do we need to make an inventory of all that is in this room?" She had no desire to talk about why she was hiding. It would be best if they just moved on to another subject that had nothing to do with broken hearts being able to crack further when presented unexpectedly with the cause of the heartbreak in the first place.

"Mrs. Nichols has a thorough inventory already made of everything – not just this room."

Kitty's brow furrowed. "Then, what do we need to do to get Netherfield ready to be vacant?"

Jane smiled sheepishly. "Very little, truth be told. Netherfield's staff is excellent, and it is not the first time the house has sat vacant for a lengthy period."

Kitty sat up. "Then, why am I here?" Mama had said it was to help Jane prepare to close Netherfield for an extended period of time. Why would Mama say that if it were not true? Unless... Well, that was a shocking thought! Was Jane truly being deceptive?

"Do you know what important day is next Thursday?"

Kitty shook her head. It was the day before they were to go to town, but other than that, she could not think of any particular significance that the day held.

"It is Mother and Father's anniversary. They will have been married twenty-four years next Thursday."

"Oh, I had forgotten it was so soon!" That was indeed a day of great importance. "Are you planning a dinner for them?" Since the time Jane was twelve, she had taken over the celebration preparations for their parent's anniversary dinner. Before that Mama had always arranged things.

"It may be the last dinner I get to plan."

Kitty gasped. "Oh, how sad!" Life was changing at such a rapid pace lately with sisters marrying and moving away. Parts of it had been exciting, while other parts such as this, brought a pang of sorrow and the dreadful feeling that she was being left behind and would be forgotten.

"In a way, it is," Jane agreed. "But in another way, it is as it should be. Parents only have their children for so long – especially if they are daughters." She rested her hand on her belly. "Even this little one will one day leave me and begin his or her own family. I will still be loved by my child, and I will miss him or her dearly. However, it would be far more sad if this child never found the happiness I have found with Charles, would it not?"

A tear slipped down Kitty's cheek. She would be one of Mama's children who would never find such happiness. She might find a sort of happiness and a pleasant prospect, but... She found herself wrapped in Jane's arms before she could do more than think of Mr. Langley.

"You are not well," Jane declared. "And do not tell me that you are, for I shall not believe it." She squeezed Kitty tighter. "Is it Mr. Langley?"

"Yes," she whispered.

Jane rubbed her back in soothing circles. She would be such a good mother. Caring was such an integral part of her very substance. "You will remember," Jane spoke only a little louder than a whisper, "that I know somewhat about disappointment in love. You can speak to me about him."

"Not while he is here." It would be enough of a struggle to maintain some sort of composure when forced to see the source of one's disappointment. To also be required to speak about him would make maintaining a façade of pleasantness utterly impossible.

"But you do like Mr. Langley?" Jane asked as she released Kitty from her embrace.

"Very much." She more than liked him. She loved him. That was why she had allowed him to kiss her when she had never, ever allowed anyone else to do so. She wanted to be his and have him as hers forever. Before she allowed him to kiss her, she had imagined him proclaiming his love to her after having kissed her, but he had not.

"But you refused him."

"Not forever." The weight which had been crushing her heart for a month lifted slightly with the admission. "I just never got to tell him that part." She drew and released a shaky breath. "However, it is just as well that I did not since he did not admire me as much as I did him."

The truth of her words stung. How easy it was to be taken in by a charming fellow!

"I should have followed Mary's lead and refused

to allow him to call on me." She sighed. "But he is so handsome, and we got on so well." It had been as if they were two parts that made a perfectly wonderful whole.

"Are you certain he does not admire you?"

"Not enough to marry me." Just enough to steal a kiss. She brushed a tear from her cheek.

"I am not so sure you are correct." The smile which accompanied Jane's word was soft and gentle. "You refused him first. He may have been allowing you to have what you said you wanted."

Could that be true?

"Charles said he looked stricken to see you in our carriage today – as if seeing you was painful."

Seeing him had been – no, *was* – painful. How she wished she could go back in time and undo what had been done. If she had not stolen away to see him in the music room. If she had not allowed him to kiss her. If Lydia had not opened that door. Maybe then, she would be in a drawing room in London with him sitting next to her and coming to love her as she loved him.

"Why did you refuse him?" Jane asked.

That was not easily explained without breaking a confidence, but she had promised Georgiana that she would not tell anyone about how she feared having to discern who was and who was not a worthy gentleman. Being an heiress was not so great a blessing as Kitty had thought it would be, for it meant a lady had to fear fortune hunters who played at being lovers when all they really loved about a lady was her money and connections.

"I am not ready to marry. There were yet two months of the season to enjoy, and I am not yet even eighteen. How could I marry so young?" That seemed a good reason for refusing to marry, did it not?

"You are older than Lydia."

"And younger than you, Elizabeth, and Mary," Kitty protested. She could not allow her argument to be so easily discounted, for she had no other reason to give for not wishing to immediately marry Mr. Langley.

"Yes, you are, but it is not all that unusual for a lady to marry when she is just eighteen, or even younger." Jane held Kitty's chin. "Especially if that lady has found someone to love most ardently and who loves her with the same devotion as Lydia has."

"Twenty is a much better age at which to marry."

For by the time she was twenty, Georgiana's first season would be over.

The comment was answered with an arched brow, accompanied by, "Shall we ask Mary about that? She does everything that is proper and yet, she is now married and will not be twenty until July."

"She was almost twenty when she married," Kitty protested weakly.

"And excessively in love and loved in return."

That was true. Lord Westonbury loved Mary madly. One did not have to wonder about his care for her, for he was always kissing her fingers and calling her his love.

"If I find such a love, then I will marry before I am twenty." It seemed a safe promise to make since it was not going to happen. Her chance had passed her by.

"Are you certain you have not found such a love?"

Kitty opened her mouth to assure her sister that she had not found anything of the kind but was interrupted by the door to the music room opening.

"Forgive me for intruding," Mr. Alfred Langley

said. "I was told Miss Bennet was in here when I was looking for her."

"You were looking for me?"

"I was. I had hoped you might join Lori and me for a walk through the garden."

"What a perfectly wonderful idea!" Jane cried with far too much excitement. Jane did not cry things. Jane spoke in hushed tones, in stern whispers, in subdued delighted surprise, and in a whole host of other softer, less exuberant ways. "I would not be opposed to joining you if you do not mind the intrusion of an old married lady."

"I am sure neither Lori nor I mind one bit," Mr. Alfred Langley replied with a laugh. "We are the ones importuning you with our sudden arrival."

"I am certain you did not plan to be stranded on the side of the road by a broken wheel. It was providence who brought you to us, and therefore, your arrival cannot be an imposition."

Kitty's mouth popped open. Jane did not tease and flutter her lashes – or at least, Kitty had never seen her do so until now. She was acting far more like Lydia or Mama than Jane. Oh! Oh, no! She was matchmaking, and that must be stopped.

"I had hoped to take a rest before dinner," Kitty said.

"You were just resting when I discovered you, so I think ten minutes before you dress should be enough to refresh you after you have taken some air." Jane gave her hand a pat.

Alfred looked from one sister to the other. "If you prefer not to..."

"We will join you," Jane interrupted as she rose from the chaise. "Kitty go get your bonnet and have mine brought to me, will you?" She turned back to Alfred. "Have you seen my husband?"

"Yes, I was just speaking with him before I came to find Miss Bennet."

"Kitty, for what are you waiting?" Jane gave a nod of her head toward the door.

Oh! Jane could be demanding at times. Kitty barely held back a displeased huff as she rose to do as she had been bid.

"Was your cousin speaking to my husband as well?" Jane had turned back to Alfred.

"No, he was occupied with writing directions to his coachman to see that a carriage is rented. He seems in a great hurry to get to town, though he did not wish to go there at all when my mother first proposed the idea to him."

Kitty stood for only a moment longer at the door to the music room, just long enough to hear Mr. Langley's cousin comment on how different his cousin seemed after his current season in town. She wished to stay and listen longer, but she dared not as she heard someone on the stairs. Therefore, without latching the door, for that would draw attention to the fact that she had been listening at the door, she hurried down the hall and to the staircase, where she found herself face to face with the other Mr. Langley. The one she had been attempting to avoid.

"Miss Bennet," he said in surprise. "I was just going to join my cousin in the garden." He pulled at his gloves, which looked to be very snuggly in place and not at all in want of adjustment.

"I know. My sister and I are to join you." She watched his face carefully. There was a slight twitch as if he had tasted something unpleasant. "I tried to allow you to be free of my presence, but my sister insisted."

His brow furrowed. "You tried what?"

"I tried to refuse."

"And you did not succeed?" His tone was derisive.

"No, Mr. Langley, I did not succeed," Kitty snapped. "Perhaps you could teach me how to refuse properly." She hurried up the stairs and away from him.

"Kitty," he called after her.

"Yes, Mr. Langley?" she brushed a tear from her cheek as she turned toward him.

He opened his mouth, closed it again, and then shook his head. "Forgive me." He looked as if he was going to climb the stairs towards her but then, he hesitated as if he had thought better of his action. "Forgive me," he repeated, and, after giving a nod of his head, he continued down the stairs.

Chapter 4

He should have walked to Meryton and delivered his message to his coachman himself. He could have taken a bag and stayed at the inn.

He paced Netherfield's entryway from stairway to door and back.

He should have offered to ride one of the horses instead of sending a groom. Even riding in the carriage with a broken wheel and risking life and limb seemed a safer option than being here – with her.

What was taking his cousin so long?

Lorcan pulled at his cravat and fidgeted with his sleeves while he paced. He needed to be somewhere – anywhere – that was not here where he could give in to his desire to run up those stairs and beg Kitty to accept him.

"Did you get your missive sent?"

Finally! Lorcan turned on his heel to find that his cousin and Mrs. Bingley had joined him.

"Yes, yes, it is sent. I expect a reply when the groom returns. Mr. Bingley was kind enough to lend him a horse so the distance will be more easily covered in a timely fashion." He shifted from foot to foot while turning his hat in his hands.

"We could wait for my sister in the drawing room," Mrs. Bingley suggested. "Though I am sure she will not be overly long in fetching our things."

Lorcan did not want to wait in the drawing room, for that would require sitting, and sitting was not a pleasant or even possible prospect at present. However, before he could concoct a rational reason as to why the entrance hall was a better option for waiting than the drawing room was, Mr. Bingley stepped into the corridor from the very room Lorcan was trying desperately to avoid.

"I thought I heard my wife," he said with a smile.

How absolutely content the man looked! Fortunate fellow.

"Are we about ready?" Bingley asked.

"We are just waiting for Kitty," his wife replied.

"Ah, very good! And there she is now."

As sure as the sun warmed the earth and

brought brightness to a grey English day, Kitty Bennet was about halfway down the stairs, and drawing ever closer, while her brother-in-law expressed his delight over having guests to fill his house even if it was only for a day or two.

"No," Lorcan said, pulling his eyes away from the lovely lady descending the stairs and turning back to the conversations around him when Bingley suggested that Alfred and he stay longer and wait for their carriage to be fixed. "We really must depart for town as soon as possible."

"I do not see why," Alfred muttered.

"Because there are things to be done before we return home." They were not things of a pressing nature per se, but it seemed the most acceptable reply since *running away from a lady* was neither the noblest thing to do nor to admit to – especially if the lady from whom a gentleman was running was standing with him.

"And our time is limited," he added. "Many will be leaving town soon to return to their country houses."

"Or to attend house parties." Alfred teased. He could be most trying at times – such as now when Lorcan was not in a mood to be jovial.

"Have you been invited to any?" Mrs. Bingley looked first at Alfred and then Lorcan.

"No, to my mother's great disappointment, only Lorcan has received any invitations – not that that is unusual. He is rather in demand. It is just one of the many joys of being a firstborn with a fortune and good connections."

"Yes, a great joy," Lorcan grumbled.

"How many parties will you be attending?" Mrs. Bingley inquired, as she took her husband's arm and nodded for Kitty to join Lorcan and Alfred.

"None."

"None?" Bingley cried. "I should think that there would be some fun to be had at a house party, or such was my experience at the two I attended. Pretty ladies, good gents, and much to keep one entertained."

"And a dozen scheming matrons to see one wed," Lorcan retorted. "Not that I am opposed to marrying," he adjusted when he saw Kitty's eyebrows rise. "I am quite in favour of the institution when there is a willingness to enter it on both sides."

"That is the challenge, is it not?" Mrs. Bingley

thankfully inserted before Lorcan felt the need to elaborate more on his views of marriage.

Why had he even mentioned it? It was likely because Kitty, since about a week after his having first met her, had often made him think of marriage.

"The garden awaits," Mrs. Bingley said.

"Please, lead on." Alfred waved his hand toward the door with a flourish, and then promptly followed behind their hosts, leaving Lorcan to do the gentlemanly thing and offer his arm to Kitty.

Kitty looked at his proffered arm and then him.

"Please," he whispered when she hesitated. As much as he feared her touch, he also craved it.

Her lips twitched upward in a brief smile before she placed her hand very lightly on his arm. With great effort, he refrained from covering her hand with his own and drawing her closer to his side.

"Have you been home for very long?" he asked as they descended Netherfield's front steps and followed a distance behind the Bingleys and Alfred.

"Just over a month."

"Truly?" He had not expected her to have left London at the same time he had.

"It was my punishment for my indecorous behaviour."

Her soft admission pierced his heart. It was his fault that she had acted as improperly as she had, for he was the one who had asked if he could kiss her and then had not stopped at a chaste one. "Forgive me. I did not mean for you to find yourself in trouble."

"That is always a possibility when one decides to misbehave."

"True, but still, I am sorry it happened – the punishment, that is." He could not bring himself to be completely sorry for having kissed her, though the memory of it, and her, tormented him daily.

"I am as well." Her cheeks coloured.

"Are you sorry for all of it, or just the punishment?" He likely should not ask such a thing, but he seemed unable to refrain. Something within him needed to know her answer.

Her eyes did not leave their observation of the ground as he and she walked with the sound of stones beneath boots punctuating the silence.

"All of it," she finally whispered before lifting her eyes from the path and looking off to the left.

At her words, the world seemed to grind to a

slow and painful halt as coldness spread from where her hand lay on his left arm to his heart, grasping and strangling him with its intensity. His fond memory of her turned to ice and crumbled in his mind's eye, taking with it any glimmer of hope he had held.

Was it possible for an otherwise healthy gentleman to die while walking due to a disappointment that could not be measured? Lorcan sucked in a breath but there was only enough room in his constricted chest for a shallow one that left him gasping for another.

"Are you well?" Kitty cried.

Mutely, he shook his head, for speech had left him.

"Do you wish to sit down?"

He nodded. Sitting was not exactly what he wished to do, but it was likely better than standing when the garden began to waver. She led him to a bench, and gratefully, he sank down onto it before his legs could fail him.

"Go on without me," he said when he could once again speak now that his mind was no longer focused so intently on keeping him upright.

"But you are unwell," she protested.

"I will be well. It must be from the knock on the head in the carriage." It was not, and he was not entirely certain he would be well. However, he did not wish for her to coddle him as if he were someone for whom she cared when she so obviously did not and never had.

"I cannot leave you. It would be most impolite."

"Please, just go. I do not want you to stay."

Kitty's eyes grew wide with horror. "If that is what you wish," she said, lifting her chin and straightening her shoulders. "Tell my sister when she finds you that I offered to stay with you, but you once again refused me. I will be in my room until you leave."

She spun away from him, but he caught her hand.

"Kindly allow me to leave you as you requested." She gave her hand a pull, causing him to grip her more firmly.

"Understand," he growled, "that you first refused me." He released her hand and turned his face away from her. "Not that any of that matters to you."

"But –"

He cut her off with a wave of his hand and a "Leave me."

"But –" she tried again only to be once again cut off. This time by a whispered "Please."

"Is it truly what you want?" she asked.

He clamped his teeth together so that he could not say what he truly longed for and gave a nod of his head. He closed his eyes as he heard first, her gasp and then, her retreating footsteps.

He would not let her lead him along again. He had willingly followed her down a happy trail before, believing that she fancied him as much as he fancied her. He would not make that mistake again. He would put his heart away and be civil but nothing more.

He once again struggled to draw a deep breath. Surely, it would become easier as time went on. It was only now when he would feel as if he had cut out his own heart with a dull blade and fed it to the crows. He rubbed his chest. He would miss his heart, for the loss of it made him feel very empty.

He bowed his head and, with eyes closed, concentrated on breathing and not dying. He had a cousin to deliver to London and to help in securing a good position. He was needed by someone – even if he was not wanted by the lady he loved.

"Where is Miss Bennet?"

"In her room," he replied without lifting his head to look at his cousin. There had not been enough footsteps for him to be accompanied by anyone.

Alfred sat down next to him. "Why is she in her room? Did you banish her?"

Lorcan shook his head. "She would rather be there than anywhere near me."

"Well, with as sullen as you have been, I am not entirely certain I blame her." He nudged Lorcan with his shoulder.

"Leave off, Alfred. Please." Lorcan rose from the bench. "I am walking to Meryton."

"You are what?"

"I am walking to Meryton. I will sleep at the inn."

"You are not walking anywhere." Alfred stood in his path. "Tell me what has you in such a state."

"No."

"If that is what you want."

"Why must everyone keep saying that?" Lorcan shouted.

Alfred took him by the shoulders, backed him up, and pushed him down onto the bench.

"I do not take kindly to being yelled at." He crossed his arms and glared down at his seated cousin. "Since you will not tell me what has you in such a foul mood, then I will have to assume it is because a certain young lady does not return your affections."

Lorcan scowled. It did not take a great genius to piece that together.

"Mrs. Bingley and I had a very enlightening conversation – which came on the heels of another rather interesting conversation that I had with Mr. Bingley. It seems, my dear crotchety cousin, that you ran into a small bit of trouble while in town this season – the sort of trouble that steals a fellow's heart and threatens to ruin his future happiness when he tries to be too noble by half."

"You know not of what you speak." How could he? Alfred may have heard about what happened in the music room at Matlock House, but he could not know how crushing the events which concluded the affair had been.

"I think I do." He straightened his sleeves. "Seeing that I am ordained, though I have not yet secured a living, I am free to counsel you."

"You? Counsel me?"

"You need not look so appalled. I assure you that Mr. Hatcher has been an excellent mentor and has even had me offer advice to several people while I was his curate."

"You are my cousin."

He nodded. "And I could be your parson if the living under your purview fell open."

"It will not be falling open any time soon."

"I am not so certain. I have heard that perhaps Dr. Miller might be offered a better position, though it would be wrong for me to give too many details." He smiled at Lorcan when he looked at Alfred in disbelief. "It seems worse to gossip about a man of the cloth than it does to listen to stories about one's cousin."

"I am sure it is not any worse. In fact, I am positive they are both equally as heinous."

"Be that as it may, it does not solve your problem."

"My problem is outside the realm of solution – even by an ordained minister — I am afraid." He attempted to rise, but Alfred pushed him down again.

"You are not leaving this bench until I have extracted a promise from you that you are not going to go running off to an inn in Meryton."

"I cannot stay here."

Alfred shook his head. "You must. You are my guardian."

"I thought I was your companion."

"You were until being a guardian and abandoning your charge seemed a worse crime than a companion leaving his post."

Lorcan shook his head at his cousin's ability to turn a situation so that it suited him best. "Very well, I promise not to abandon you."

Alfred stepped back a step so that Lorcan could rise. "And I," he said, "promise not to help you find a wife as I did my brother unless it becomes absolutely necessary."

Chapter 5

Kitty tossed her bonnet on the chair next to her dressing table, slipped off her boots, and sat down heavily on the floral upholstered chair near the window. The breeze felt cool as it brushed the tears on her cheeks. The grumble of Mr. Langley's voice as he reminded her of her rejection would not leave her mind. It kept repeating while the image of him turning away from her wavered on the tears that filled her eyes and spilled down her cheeks.

A mew drew her attention to the tabby rubbing his side against her leg. She reached down and gave the cat's ears a scratch.

"I think Jane was right, Oliver," she whispered.

Oliver tilted his head toward her hand and purred.

"But how can I not be sorry all of this has happened?"

Oliver continued to ignore everything about Kitty except for the hand which scratched his ears.

"I just want everything to return to how it was before Mary got married." She flopped backwards in the chair and looked at the ceiling. "But it will not."

Oliver mewed, but not in agreement or because he was paying any attention to what Kitty was saying. No, he was less than pleased that she had stopped scratching him. He rubbed against her leg again before leaving her alone and stalking the room.

Kitty watched him slink along the wall and pounce at the curtain when it fluttered in the breeze.

"No, Oliver." She rose and removed the fabric from his claws before he could cause too much damage by kneading it between his paws. She turned him away from the window and went to the dresser to fetch a fresh handkerchief.

She dried her face, looked in the mirror, and went to the basin of water to attempt to wash away the evidence of her sorrow. It did a little good, but only just a little. She splashed water on her face once more after a second perusal of her appearance in the mirror. As she patted her face dry with a towel, she looked for Oliver. Perhaps if she were to snuggle him next to her on the bed, she would feel somewhat comforted. She had often found doing so with one of the cats at home had always had a calming effect.

"Oliver," she called when she could not find him immediately. There was a soft thud on the carpet behind her. She spun to see the contents of her box of ribbons scattered across the floor and one ribbon making its way out of the room in Oliver's possession.

"Come back with that!" She dashed out the door, which she had left open the smallest bit so that Oliver could come and go without disturbing her from her repose. She had not thought that he would use the opening to abscond with one of her ribbons!

Oliver scampered down the stairs with Kitty following behind.

"Pardon me," she said as she passed Mr. Langley who was on his way up the stairs.

"Oliver!"

Calling to him did not produce the desired

result, for Oliver only paused for a moment before racing away and into the front drawing room.

"Oh, how am I supposed to get you when you are under that?" Kitty gave a small stamp of her stockinged foot.

Oliver had slipped under a chest of drawers that held a clock, a lamp, and a beautiful vase that stood, waiting for a fresh bouquet of flowers.

She got down on her hands and knees and peeked under the piece of furniture.

"May I please have my ribbon?" she begged in as sweet a voice as she could muster when feeling as annoyed as she did. She could reach him if she were to lie on the floor and stick her arm all the way under the set of drawers, but she had no desire for her hand to be scratched or bitten.

"If you will allow me, I think I might be able to help you."

Kitty sat back on her heels. "He is all the way at the back."

"I am sure I can reach that far." Mr. Langley knelt next to her and then lay down on the floor.

Kitty grabbed his arm before he stuck it under the cabinet. "He might bite you."

"I am wearing a jacket and gloves." He held her

gaze. "And it would not be the first time I have been bitten by a cat while retrieving a ribbon."

"It is not?" How often did one come across a cat who was a ribbon thief?

"As you know, I have a sister." His voice was muffled a bit by his position as he reached under the cabinet. "And she has this dreadful beast who steals everything, though he seems to prefer things which are yellow – as does my sister. There now, be a good lad and let go of the ribbon. Miss Kitty does not want her ribbon shredded." He turned to smile at her. "Do you?"

Kitty bit back a giggle and shook her head.

"Ah, there we go." Mr. Langley pulled his hand and the ribbon out in triumph. "One grateful ivory ribbon." He held it out to her. "Safe and sound and ready to tie up your hair when you wear your green muslin."

"You know I wear this with my green muslin?"

"You wore it the first day we went driving in the park," he said as he pushed up from the floor.

"You remember what I wore to the park?"

Mr. Langley nodded. "I like green, and it suits you. Of course, I do not remember seeing you wear anything which did not suit you."

How did a gentleman who could remember what a lady wore not be attached to the lady? She remembered everything he had worn, which was not something she could say for any other gentleman.

"I have never seen you wear anything which did not suit you either." She wound the ribbon she held around her fingers.

"Thank you. I like to think I have a good eye, and Westonbury assures me I do. However, it is nice to hear it from a lady and not a gentleman." His lips tipped up on one side in that charming way they often did when he was sounding confident but looking just the smallest bit embarrassed.

He rose from the floor and extended a hand to assist her in the most natural fashion as if they had not just argued in the garden.

"Thank you for retrieving my ribbon," she said as she gained her footing. He was standing so close to her, much as he had been when they were in the music room at Matlock House before he kissed her. The thought caused her to take a step away from him. "I should go put this away and clean up the other ribbons that Oliver scattered on the floor."

"Yes, you would not want him to steal another."

The space between them was once again growing awkward. The air seemed to grow heavy as if it was laden with something which was either ominous or wonderful.

"No, I would not want him to do that, for how would I get it back?" She should go to her room now, but that whatever it was which hung between them seemed to have wrapped its hands around her ankles and was holding her in place.

Mr. Langley looked as if he wanted to say something but would not. How she hated that they could not speak freely to one another as they had when in town before that awful day.

"This is why I regret it." Her thought popped out of her mouth unbidden. She pressed her lips together and took another step away from him and toward the door. "Forgive me. I should see to my ribbons." Once her feet were moving, they seemed unable to stop, and she nearly flew from the room.

"Wait," he called, racing up the stairs after her. "Please."

She stopped when she got to the landing on the floor where her room was located.

"Why?" she asked. She knew why he wished for her to wait. She did not know why she was even asking such a silly question. A lady could not blurt out a thought about something about which she and a gentleman had argued and not understand that he was likely curious to know what her random thought had meant.

"What did you mean just now that this is why you regret it? What do you regret, and what is your reason for the regret?"

Below them, a clock chimed the half-hour.

"My sister will be returning from her walk soon, and I must get ready for dinner. We will eat in half an hour."

"Kitty, please," he begged.

Her heart sighed its desire at his use of her Christian name. It had always sounded so much sweeter falling from his lips than anyone else's.

"What did you mean? What do you regret?"

She blew out a breath and willed herself not to run away instead of answering. Dread filled her now just as it had when he had asked her about her regret in the garden. She still remembered his kiss fondly. She dreamt of it nearly every night. Its memory caused her to cry into her pillow. But more painful than the recollection of that sweet stolen moment was the loss of everything which had come before it.

"I regret allowing you to kiss me." She tried to keep her eyes on him. However, it was too difficult, and she looked away just as she had in the garden.

"Why?" The question she had expected him to ask her in the garden came in a whisper.

"Because..." she shrugged. How did one put this into words? "So much was lost because of it."

He took a step closer to her. "What was lost?"

Again, she blew out a breath and willed herself not to turn and run. "Us. Our friendship."

He took her hands, gripping them as tightly as one might do to keep someone from falling from a precipice.

The door below them opened.

"I must go," she pulled on her hands.

"But you refused me."

"And you refused me," she replied, once again giving her hands a tug. This time he released them.

"Why?" he asked.

She shook her head. "I must go. It would not do to have my sister find us here like this." She turned away from him.

He followed her two steps down the hallway.

"You are not going to stay in your room until I am gone, are you?"

"No. Jane would never allow it."

"But do you want to?"

She stopped and nodded without turning around. "It would be easier."

"Easier than what?" he pressed.

She looked over her shoulder at him. "It would be easier than being reminded of what was lost." Even if it had been a foolish fantasy, and he had not loved her as she thought he had.

"I will go see if Lori is still here and has not wandered off to Meryton." Mr. Alfred Langley's voice floated up the stairs.

"Were you going to Meryton?" Kitty asked.

"I considered it." He looked nervously down the stairs. She knew just as he did that, soon, his cousin would make the turn at the next landing and discover them.

"Why?" she whispered.

"You should go to your room." He turned to go in the opposite direction.

"Why?" she whispered again. This time more earnestly.

He stopped and turned back towards her. "For

the same reason you would rather stay in your room. Now, go before he sees us. He can be insufferable. Perhaps we can discuss this more later?"

Kitty nodded as, for the first time in more than a month, a real, happy smile spread from her heart to her lips. Perhaps it had not been such a foolish fantasy after all.

Chapter 6

Blasted Alfred! Lorcan grumbled to himself for the fourth time since they had all gathered in the drawing room before dinner. His cousin, it appeared, had appointed himself as guardian of Lorcan.

"I am not going to leave. You can move a few feet away from me," Lorcan whispered to the annoyance at this side. How was he to have any time to speak with Kitty if Alfred insisted on being his shadow.

"Oh, I know you are not, for I am not going to allow it."

"I have assured you several times that you do not need to fret over my walking to Meryton. I am far too tired to walk that far at this hour of the day."

"There are horses in the stable."

"I have no plan to borrow a horse. I intend to wait right here, surrounded by the comfort Netherfield offers, until such time as my carriage comes to collect us. You *can* move away from me."

His cousin grimaced and shook his head. "I am afraid I cannot."

Kitty, who was in close conversation with her sister, glanced at him as he entered the drawing room behind Bingley.

Bingley turned to Alfred and Lorcan when they were just inside the room and said, as he motioned to some empty chairs, "It is my wife's doing I am afraid. She finds disagreements to be disagreeable, and I find disagreeing with her to be even more dis-agreeable."

"As you should."

Lorcan glowered at his cousin, who responded far too readily. "I am not usually the argumentative sort. I am actually rather amiable."

Only Alfred remained to hear his protest as Bingley had deserted them to join his wife on the sofa across from them.

Or, that is, Lorcan had thought it was only his cousin who heard his protest until he heard a sweet voice say, "Yes, you are."

"Thank you."

Kitty, whose cheeks bore the prettiest shade of

embarrassment for having told Lorcan he was indeed amiable, turned back to her sister. "Jane, I was going to tell you that while you were in the garden –"

"Oliver!" Bingley interrupted Kitty's comment as he plucked the cat from the top of the table next to him. "Cats do not belong on tables." He put the creature on the floor.

"Cats enjoy most the places they should not be," Mrs. Bingley said with a laugh. "How many times has one or another of the cats at Longbourn been found on top of a table or sitting on a shelf, Kitty?"

"I am sure I have not counted, but it drives Mama to distraction at times," Kitty replied. "However, for the most part, they are good and do not destroy things."

"Oliver has not yet learned that skill," Bingley grumbled.

"He is just a kitten, Charles. He will learn or grow bored. Either way, our house will soon be safe from his antics."

Bingley cast a skeptical look at the kitten that was rubbing against his leg and purring.

"Do you regret giving him to me?"

Bingley's eyes grew wide. "No, no, my dear, I do

not," he hurried to assure her. "I do regret the broken vases and missing trinkets."

"Some of those trinkets are under that dresser." Lorcan pointed to the piece of furniture standing against the wall to the right of the door.

Bingley's eyebrows rose. "Indeed?"

"That is what I was trying to tell you," Kitty said. "Oliver stole my ribbon earlier when you were in the garden, but Mr. Langley came to its rescue and retrieved it for me. It was the ivory one I purchased when we went shopping in Meryton with Miss Darcy. It goes so well with my green muslin that I would be very sorry to lose it." Her lips quirked into a small smile, and she glanced at Lorcan.

"It would be a disappointment," Alfred replied. "Or, I imagine it would be."

"I have a sister, who is rather fond of ribbons, and I can assure you that the loss of a favourite embellishment is indeed a disappointment," Lorcan said.

"I can attest to that as well," Bingley inserted. "Caroline was never so attached to her fripperies as Louisa, but they both could become excessively irritable when one had to be replaced since one could never quite find the same thing with which one had become accustomed."

"Oh, most certainly!" Kitty cried. "I should think I might be able to find this same ribbon in the store as it has not been too long since I purchased it and since there was a good length of it there. However, there is no guarantee that it has not all been purchased, and who knows if the proprietor will get another order of exactly the same ribbons." Her expression grew serious. "And the shade of ivory might vary from one lot to another. The shade is very important, you know. I would not want it to be too yellow, after all."

Bingley nodded as if he did indeed know.

"My sister is fond of colour," Mrs. Bingley inserted. "She is the most artistic of us all and has the best eye for these things, though I beg of you not to mention it to Lydia, for she will protest it quite vehemently."

"Lydia is very good with fashion. Much better than I," Kitty said.

Mrs. Bingley patted Kitty's knee. "I think you are likely equals in that."

"Oh, no," Kitty assured her. "I must defer to our sister and Miss Darcy when it comes to the best sense of fashion. I assure you that I have learned much from them both."

She was so willing to praise others. Lorcan had noticed that about her from their first meeting, for during that first dance, she had commented on the elegance of the décor in the room, as well as at least one lady's gown.

He also knew that she did indeed have an eye for beautiful objects and could, much to his delight, express the emotion each stirred. He had never before called on a lady who had spoken about the calm, serenity of a particular shade of blue or the liveliness of the yellow in a painting, and her ability to emotionally connect to things of beauty was not limited to visual works of art, for he had seen her dab at her eyes when listening to Miss Darcy play the piano. In this way, he and she were kindred spirits. However, she was fortunate to be a lady and had, therefore, more freedom to express her emotional responses as it was more acceptable for a lady to require a handkerchief during a musical performance than it was for a gentleman.

"Whether it was your choice or the suggestion of another," Lorcan said to Kitty, "your choice of ribbon is excellent, and I was happy to save it from

Oliver." Three sets of curious eyes turned toward him. "Ivory compliments green very nicely." He resisted the urge to run a finger around his collar. "I quite like green. It is perhaps my favourite colour."

The comment seemed to do little to relieve his companions' curiosity, but he was not about to explain anything further about how Kitty and the incident with that ivory ribbon had impacted his current, tentatively happy state.

Grasping hold of an idea to turn his comments about ribbons and colours into something of use and a source of discussion to replace the silence which was currently reigning in the drawing room, he turned to Bingley and asked, "Do you have a colour you prefer above others?"

Truly, he did not care what colour was Bingley's favourite. As a matter of fact, he only wished to hear Kitty's reply. It was not as if he did not know what she would say, for he had discovered that bit of information during their five weeks together in town. His reason for wishing to hear her response was that he just wanted to hear her speak to him as she had before any rejections had happened. His desire to reclaim what had been was palpable, and after their short exchange in the hall upstairs earlier this evening, he was hopeful that it was not an impossibility to return to some sort of relationship that went beyond mere friendship.

"I would have to say," Bingley replied, "that I prefer whatever colour my wife is wearing, which means that tonight I prefer blue."

Mrs. Bingley rolled her eyes but from the smile that graced her face, Lorcan could tell she was flattered. It was lovely to see a gentleman still flirting with his lady after she had become his wife. His father and mother rarely flirted, but Lord and Lady Matlock engaged in the practice now and again. And, he thought with a smile, he was certain that Westonbury would not give up flirting with Kitty's sister, Mary, even though he was now married to her.

"I often wear blue because my husband prefers it," Mrs. Bingley said.

"Such a sacrificial lady I have found!" Bingley cried, lifting his wife's hand to his lips.

"It is fortunate that I also prefer blue, so I have several dresses which are that colour," she continued while attempting not to look flustered.

"And you, Miss Bennet? What is your preferred colour?" Lorcan asked.

She sighed and looked perplexed. "I find it so hard to choose just one, but while I do enjoy certain shades of green, I find I am often drawn to things which are purple. There is just something about the colour which captures my attention."

"It is a lovely colour," he assured her before turning to his cousin. "And you?"

"Black," Alfred said simply.

"Black?" Kitty echoed in surprise.

"Yes, black."

"Why?" It seemed as if Kitty was finding it challenging to comprehend someone preferring black.

"Why not?" Alfred replied.

"It... it... it just seems such a dreary colour. One could not paint a wall black or plant a border of black flowers."

"I will grant you that," Alfred replied. "However, consider how nearly every other color can be enhanced by placing it next to something which is black. Take red, yellow, and white as examples – they all become brighter when contrasted with black. Just think of the night sky. Do we see as many stars when the moon is bright as we do when the moon is absent?"

"I had not thought of that."

Lorcan loved the way Kitty's brow furrowed while a small smile pulled at her lips. She was obviously delighted by the images his cousin had created.

"And," Alfred continued, "it is the ultimate colour of love."

Lorcan's attention snapped to his cousin. "How is black the colour of love?"

"Indeed, I am curious about that as well," Mrs. Bingley inserted.

"What colour do you wear when someone dies?"

"Black," Bingley answered.

"Precisely."

"But does that not make it the colour of sorrow?" Kitty leaned forward. Curiosity filled her eyes.

Alfred held up a finger to punctuate his words as a professor might do when challenging his pupils "It is both, but why?"

"Yes, that is what I would like to know!" Kitty cried.

"I think I know," Lorcan said as an image of his grandmother came to mind.

"Then tell us, cousin. Why is black both the colour of love and of sorrow?"

"Because," Lorcan said while, with some difficulty, he kept his eyes on his cousin, "without love there is no sorrow."

He glanced quickly in Kitty's direction. He loved her. To the very depths of his soul he loved her, for his sorrow at having given her up – though he believed with all that was within him that it was what she had wanted — had consumed him completely. Not an area of his life had not been coloured by the dark hues of sorrow after their parting.

"Oh." Kitty sank back on the sofa as if overwhelmed by the thought.

"Is that the answer?" Bingley asked.

Alfred nodded. "Our grandmother," he motioned to Lorcan and then himself, "has never donned a colour other than black since our grandfather died five years ago. I asked her about it once, and she told me it was because she loved my grandfather so greatly."

Lorcan nodded. He had heard her say something similar to his mother when his mother had suggested choosing a different coloured fabric for a new gown that was being ordered.

From there, as Lorcan contemplated his love for

the lady across from him and the surprising astuteness of his cousin, the conversation turned to relations and which were favoured, and which were avoided, before moving on to other topics before draughts and fox and geese were brought out.

While Mr. and Mrs. Bingley settled in to play draughts, Lorcan was given the privilege to play fox and geese with Kitty. It would have been a wonderful way to get to speak to her in hushed tones had not his annoying and ever-present cousin been at his elbow instructing him about which was an excellent move, and which was a daft one.

Finally, after several rounds of games and exchanges of partners and boards, the evening drew to a close without one private word being said to Kitty, and Lorcan ended the night as he began it, with an unmet curiosity about what happiness his future might hold.

Entering his room, Lorcan found a missive on this dresser.

"I did not wish to interrupt your game, sir," the footman, who had been assigned to assist him, said. "I was assured that it was not urgent."

And it was not. The repair to the carriage wheel

had not been too difficult and with a bit of extra coin, the vehicle would be ready to carry him and Alfred to London in the morning.

"Will you see that my cousin also sees this?"

"Of course, sir."

Lorcan held the missive out to the footman.

"Now, sir?"

Lorcan nodded. There was no need to delay the wretched news. "I can see to getting into bed on my own."

If only he had not sent that note asking for his coachman to rent a carriage so they could depart as soon as possible, then, he might have time to talk to Kitty at some point during the day tomorrow. But as it was, his earlier impatience had rendered that impossible.

"Are you certain, sir?"

"The water is warm?" He nodded to the wash-stand.

"Yes."

"Then, please wake me in the morning so that I have ample time to prepare for my journey."

He untied his cravat as the man hurried from the room with the message for Alfred. His head tipped as a thought struck him. Perhaps there was something he could do.

He tossed his jacket on the bed and opened the desk near the wardrobe. Ah, there was paper and a pen! He opened the bottle of ink, dipped his pen inside, and discovered, much to his dismay, that the bottle was empty. How could he leave Kitty a message without ink to write it? He could ask for ink, but...

He sighed and took off his waistcoat. He had dismissed his borrowed man for the night and was unwilling to call for him so soon after sending him away. He would just have to attempt to speak with Kitty before he left tomorrow.

He set about removing the rest of his clothing and had just about completed the task – only his breeches remained on his person — when there was a soft knock at his door. He pulled his shirt over his head and went to see who it was. He hoped it was Kitty and not his cousin – not that he truly expected Kitty to come knocking at his door, but a fellow could dream.

Opening the door, he found the hall empty. He stepped out and looked one way and then another. To his left, he heard a door click closed in the family wing. Perhaps it had been Kitty, but she had come to her senses before he opened the door.

He shook his head. No. That couldn't be. He had likely just heard something somewhere and thought it was at his door.

He turned to reenter his room, but then, with a smile on his face, he glanced once more toward the family rooms before untying the black ribbon which hung on the doorknob.

Chapter 7

The following morning, as Kitty placed her cup of tea back on its saucer, she felt thankful that Jane had chosen this morning to discuss their plans for the dinner for Mama and Papa, for it gave her something about which to think that was not Mr. Langley.

"Pralines," she suggested. "We simply must have pralines for Mama."

"I shall see if filbert pralines are possible," Jane said as she added the item to her list. She lifted her head and smiled. "Good morning, gentlemen."

Kitty's reprieve from thinking about Mr. Langley was at an end for him and his cousin had just entered the breakfast room.

"Did you sleep well?" Kitty's heart beat rapidly and her face felt warm as she wondered if Mr. Langley had found the ribbon she had tied to his door.

She had almost decided against knocking, but she had managed to find enough courage to rap at his door before running away to her room.

"I slept very well," Alfred replied.

Kitty was happy to hear that, of course, but she was more interested in his cousin's reply. "And you, Mr. Langley? Did you also sleep well?"

He smiled.

How good it was to see him smile – really smile, from his lips all the way up to his eyes! It was an expression which she had not realized she had missed seeing so much as she now knew she had.

"Surprisingly, I did. I had thought my mind might make it impossible, but it did not."

"Was there something pressing on your mind?" Alfred asked.

"Yes."

"Was it anything of interest?"

Lorcan lowered the teapot from which he had just filled his cup and put it back in the center of the small breakfast table. Then, lifting his cup, he held Kitty's gaze while replying, "It was of great interest to me."

"And you are not going to tell me, are you?"

Lorcan rolled his eyes, causing Kitty to giggle.

He had not been exaggerating when he had said his cousin could be an annoyance. It rather reminded her of Lydia, for her youngest sister could be a downright bother when there was something she wished to know.

"No, I am not going to tell you."

"That is a pity," Alfred muttered as he began eating his breakfast.

At least, Mr. Alfred Langley seemed willing to let the matter pass with a simple *no* as the accepted answer. Lydia would likely not be so obliging.

"I am happy to hear that you both slept well," Mrs. Bingley said. "My husband should be back from his ride soon. He was sorry that he had not mentioned that he goes riding each morning to either of you last night before we retired because he would have welcomed your company."

"A ride in the morning is a fine way to start the day," Lorcan agreed. "However, I find riding and then having to climb into a carriage shortly after to not be a favourite combination of activities."

"Oh, are you leaving us this morning?" Jane asked with interest.

"Yes, I received word that my carriage is repaired and that it would come to collect us before the day is half done. If I know my coachman as well as I think I do, I would expect he will be here by ten."

Kitty looked at the clock on the mantle. Ten? That was little more than an hour from now. "So soon?"

"I fear so, Miss Bennet."

That was disappointing. She did not have very long to find out what she needed to know.

"A walk in the garden after you have eaten might be a pleasant thing before climbing into a carriage," Kitty suggested.

Maybe if she were to walk with him in the garden, she could discover his thoughts regarding the ribbon she had left for him. She had dared to hope last evening, when speaking about his cousin's favourite colour, that the way he looked at her when he said, "without love there is no sorrow," meant that he might still love her. Oh, how she hoped that was true.

"I am not certain I will be able to join you since I usually have a cup of tea with Mr. Bingley upon his return," Jane said, "but I see no reason why you cannot accompany the Mr. Langleys on a walk, Kitty."

No! Not the Mr. Langleys. She did not want to

walk with both of them. She only wished to walk with one.

"A capital idea!" Alfred exclaimed.

It would have to do, she supposed. There might still be a moment during their walk when Mr. Alfred Langley would be distracted, and she would get to say something privately to his cousin. Yes, that would be for what she would hope – for Mr. Alfred Langley to be distracted.

"We interrupted you as you were talking about pralines," Lorcan said. "Was there a reason that sweets were needed?"

"You must not tell anyone," Kitty said, "but we are planning a special dinner party for my mother and father."

"Are you indeed?" He looked duly impressed while also seeming curious.

"For nearly as long as I can remember, Jane has been in charge of this dinner."

"And this year, I have asked Kitty to help me. She has an aptitude for these things," Jane said.

"Oh, I am not so good at it as you are!"

"No, you are better. Why do you think I asked you to help me?"

"Do you truly think so?" Kitty knew she was

good at helping plan things, but she had never considered herself to be exceptional. "Lydia always brushes my ideas aside."

Jane nodded. "Yes, she does, but then, Lydia often brushes everyone's ideas aside save for her own. But when I was asked to decide –" for that was how the argument between Kitty and Lydia was usually resolved "–how many times did I take your suggestion over Lydia's?"

"Rather often."

"And why do you suppose that is?"

"I guess I have never really thought about it much — other than to gloat over Lydia's not getting her way." She shook her head. "That makes me sound dreadful, does it not? I am certain Mary would scold me for such thoughts."

Jane laughed. "Mary has a fondness for scolding."

"That is true," Kitty agreed. "Although, lately, she seems less fond of it than she used to be."

"Lord Westonbury has had a pleasing effect on her, or so Lizzy says."

"Mary is so happy," Kitty muttered. How she wished to be so happy as Mary. She peeked at Mr.

Langley. If he loved her and would wait for her, she could be just as happy as any of her sisters were.

"Westonbury seems equally as happy, or he did the last time I saw him," Lorcan said.

"I had forgotten that you and Lord Westonbury were such good friends," Jane said. "He and Mary will be coming to this dinner, or so we hope."

"If I might ask without being too forward," Alfred said. "Why are you having a dinner in your parents' honour?"

"Oh, that is no secret," Jane assured her guests. "Twenty-four years ago, on the second Thursday from today, our parents were married. Our mother started the tradition of a special dinner on that day, and as soon as we girls were old enough to take it on, we did. Being the eldest, it has fallen to me to organize every year since then with the assistance of my sisters. This year, as you can see, I am reduced to just one assistant, but," Jane leaned forward and lowered her voice, "I have been left with the best one." She looked at Kitty. "And I will not hear a word otherwise." She sat up straight again. "For instance, I would have not thought of the filbert pralines, which are our mother's most favourite treat, but Kitty would not forget such a thing."

Goodness! It was lovely to be so praised. If it were not that she knew Jane did not flatter and fib to puff others up, Kitty might doubt the compliment; however, since it was Jane, she had no choice but to believe it.

"I find it difficult to forget that which makes another's face light up as Mama's will when we give her a small sack of her favourite treats."

"Oh, yes! We must stitch a few pockets for the praline parcels."

"Oh, and we should tie them up like a beggar's purse and set them on each plate. It will look quite festive." Who would not like to find a present waiting for them at the table even before the soup was served? Kitty knew she would find it quite delightful.

"You see, gentlemen," Jane said as she wrote down Kitty's instructions. "This is the reason I am happy to have Kitty's help."

"Yes, I can see how her creativity and attention to what makes other's happy would be a boon to you."

Ah, that — Kitty's heart sang with pleasure —

that compliment was even more gratifying than Jane's had been, for it was delightful beyond compare for a lady to hear herself lauded by the gentleman she loved and whom she hoped loved her in return.

"You should fetch your bonnet, Kitty. It appears our guests have finished their breakfast while we were talking."

"Do you wish to go to the garden now?" Kitty hoped they did, for if they put the activity off for too long, they might not get a chance to walk in the garden at all.

"I am agreeable to that."

Lorcan had answered first! That was a good sign, was it not? For did it not mean he was as eager to walk together as she was?

"I shall not be long." She rose from her chair and hurried from the room before dashing up the stairs and down the hall to her room to grab her bonnet and make certain she looked her best.

She was just exiting her room to fly back down the stairs when she saw him, standing in the hall, near the top of the stairs.

"I wished to retrieve my hat," he held up two hats, one stacked on top of the other. "I told Alfred

I would get his as well." He was breathing more pronouncedly than normal. "I had to take the stairs two at a time and run from one room to the other so that I would not miss seeing you."

Joy tugged her lips upward. "You wished to see me?"

He nodded. "Alone." He glanced down the stairs. "We do not have long, but I did not wish to leave today without at least a moment to speak to you."

"I felt the same."

"Could we begin again?"

Her brow furrowed. "How do you mean?"

"Would you allow me to court you?"

Surely, her heart was going to burst with happiness. "Oh, yes! If you truly wish to."

"More than almost anything," he replied on a sigh.

Almost anything? A small bit of happiness fled for that did not sound promising.

"My greatest desire would be to marry you."

Her eyes grew wide. Did he wish to marry her? "But you said –"

"Yes, I said what I thought I must to give you

what you wanted." He shrugged. "You had refused me." He swallowed. "Would you still refuse me?"

Her heart sank. Happiness had been within her reach and now... Oh, she did not wish to refuse him. However, she had promised Georgiana, and what kind of a friend and sister would she be if she abandoned Georgiana? Her duty to her friend must come before her own desires. Therefore, she nodded. "I would. But," she added quickly before his look of pain could deepen, "that does not mean I do not want to marry you."

"I do not understand."

"I want to marry you, I truly do, but I just cannot, at least, not yet." She wanted to reach out and caress his cheek, to smooth the look of sorrow from his face. How he must love her to look so – for without love, there was no sorrow, was that not what he had said?

"I still do not understand. Why can you not marry me yet?"

She gave in to her desire and placed her hand gently on his cheek. "I cannot tell you."

"Kitty." The word was spoken as a plea. "Did the ribbon you left me mean what I think it means?"

She nodded. Should she say it? Should she

admit to loving him before he admitted he loved her?

"Do you love me?" he asked, putting an end to her deliberation over what she should do.

She stroked his cheek as she nodded. "Yes, I love you." And she would for all time. She knew it. She just knew that he was the one with whom she wished to spend all her days. "Please," she begged, "please just court me. There is no need to rush into marriage."

"I love you, Kitty. Is that not enough of a reason to wish to give you my name? Could you not just agree to marry me, and we can plan to marry whenever you wish?" He took her hand from his cheek and kissed it before wrapping it in his hand and keeping it there.

"I..." she tipped her head and studied his face. "I never thought of that. May I have some time to consider it so that I can be certain that it would not cause me to break my promise?"

"What promise?"

Her eyes grew wide. She had not meant to mention her promise. "I cannot say." She pulled her lip between her teeth.

"What are you hiding?"

"It is nothing dreadful, and I would tell you if it was only I who would be affected. However, I cannot betray the trust of another."

"Another gentleman?" His features grew hard.

"No! Never. There is no one but you."

His expression softened.

"It is the confidence of a friend. I likely should not even tell you that much as you might guess it. Please, do not ask me to say more."

Still holding her hand, he took a step towards her, leaving only the span of their clasped hands between them. "You love me?"

She nodded and swallowed. He was looking at her as he had in the music room at Matlock House before he had kissed her, and that look was stirring a longing in her to be held by him which was nearly overwhelming.

The hats he held made a soft thud when they hit the floor, and the hand which was holding hers released her hand and wrapped around her to the small of her back. His head tilted as he leaned forward.

"Lori!"

"Blast!" Lorcan grumbled, releasing her and stepping back instead of kissing her. "He will come to find me if I do not go down." He picked up his discarded hats and extended his arm to her. "Shall we go down together?"

She did not wish to go anywhere. She wanted to stay right here with his arms around her and his lips on hers. Unfortunately, that was neither feasible nor wise. So, instead of replying as she wished, she said, "Of course," and placed her hand on his arm.

"When you arrive in town, may I call on you to hear your answer?" he asked as they took their first step down the staircase.

"You may."

"Where will you be?"

"I am not entirely certain, but I believe I am to rejoin Miss Darcy, which would mean I will be at Darcy House."

"Then, in two week's time, I will call on you at Darcy House, and, if the weather is fine, I will take you for a drive so that you can give me your answer."

Chapter 8

Lorcan poked the leg of the table next to which he sat with the toe of his boot as he made himself more comfortable in a chair at his club. Seven more days in town, waiting for Kitty to return, was going to be dreadfully long.

"You have not come to see me." A none-too-pleased Lord Westonbury took the seat across from him.

"How did you know I was in town?" Lorcan had not told anyone that he was returning – mainly because he had not wished for Kitty to know, but also because he was in no hurry to see his blissfully married friend and hear the lecture that he knew he would receive.

"How indeed?"

Westonbury leveled a severe scowl at Lorcan. It

seemed he was about to receive at least a portion of the lecture he had hoped to avoid.

"I did not even know you had left town until you had been gone a week." His friend's left eyebrow cocked. "And the mail service must be especially poor at present for I received no letter."

"I am not in the habit of writing you letters," Lorcan protested.

"That is because we are so often together and privy to the plans of the other."

"You are married. Things must necessarily change."

Westonbury crossed his arms. "I should have thought you would have informed me of your inane decision to *not* marry Kitty."

Lorcan cast a glance around the room. It was not overly full, but that did not matter. It only took one interested ear, attached to a wagging tongue, to have his business circulated throughout the beau monde. "Do you remember when we were here discussing your wife when she first arrived in town?"

Westonbury nodded.

"Remember how you said that this was not the place for certain conversations?"

Again, his friend nodded.

"Then, allow me not to reply while we are here."

"If you had called on me, I would not need to ask you here."

Why was he surrounded by such obstinate people? Westonbury could be as annoying as Alfred, who, thankfully, had taken a place at a table in the card room and left him in peace for an hour.

Lord Westonbury shifted forward and lowered his voice. "Why did you give up so easily? Do you not love her?"

Lorcan closed his eyes and shook his head. He was not going to be able to put Westonbury off as easily as his cousin.

"I gave her what she wanted." He blew out a breath. "Or what I thought she wanted." As it had turned out, he had been most decidedly wrong about what he had thought she wanted.

Westonbury's lips tipped up into a smirk. "Mrs. Bingley told Mary in the letter my wife received today that Miss Bennet seemed in much better spirits after your departure from Netherfield. Can I assume you were able to work out your differences?"

"Is that why you are here? You knew I was in town, and you came to find me?"

Wes nodded. "You were not at home, so I assumed you would be here. I am the curious sort, you know."

Oh, he knew that! Lord Westonbury was always curious to know what was or was not happening in the lives of those he counted as close friends. It was just one of the trials a fellow had to bear to be allowed such a close acquaintance with the likes of Wes.

Although it was annoying to have the fellow interested in one's affairs, it was not too great a price to pay for the fierce loyalty one received in return. It was, however, that fierceness to Wes's nature that had kept Lorcan from seeking him out immediately, for he feared that his friend would be beyond angry with him for having refused to marry the lady who was now Wes's sister through mar-riage and whom Lorcan had compromised.

"Does your father still have a living in his purview that is soon to be vacant? For that is why I am in town. My cousin is in need of a position, and I am to introduce him to a few men of influence."

"The last I heard, he does. However, you have not answered my question."

"That is because I do not know the answer. We parted amicably, but I do not have her answer."

Wes's head tipped. "Her answer to what?"

"My offer." Lorcan drained the remaining wine from his glass.

"Of marriage?"

He nodded.

"That seems promising."

It was. With any luck, Kitty would accept him. While he would rather make her his wife sooner rather than later, he was willing to wait until later so long as she promised that later would eventually arrive.

"I hear you are to travel to Netherfield next week," Lorcan said in an attempt to turn the conversation away from himself.

"Indeed, it seems I am."

"Will you be returning to town from there or continuing on to Matlock?"

"Will you still be in town?" Wes countered.

Lorcan nodded. "Until the bitter end of the season unless I see my cousin situated before then with both a living and a wife."

As expected, that information was met with a laugh.

"My aunt, Alfred's mother, is desperate to see that her last born is married and has a living which can sustain him and her future grandchildren."

If only Alfred were so eager as his mother was to see himself well-settled. Unfortunately, while Lorcan's cousin was keen to find a living, he was not so enthusiastic about getting married.

They had attended a soiree last night, and Lorcan had to admit that his cousin was not without good prospects for he was readily welcomed by several matrons and their charges. However, Alfred had only found the ladies with whom he had spoken to be tolerably interesting but not compelling, and Lorcan had to agree that a compelling lady was precisely the best sort to find – provided, of course, that such a lady was free to give her heart. Once again, he found himself wondering what promise Kitty had made and to whom.

"We are going to the theatre tomorrow," Wes said, interrupting Lorcan's thoughts about a very compelling young lady. "There is room in our box for you and your cousin. Darcy will be there with his wife and sister, and, of course, Richard and Lydia, as well as my mother and father, will also be there."

"How is your brother?"

"Well enough to discuss plans with Father for improvements to Beaumont Park and to help Lydia select the proper lace for a wedding gown."

Lorcan chuckled. "Your brother is selecting lace?"

"It is truly amazing the change in him," Wes said as he nodded. "But then, the right lady can have that effect on a gentleman."

That was true. Loving a lady did cause a gentleman to begin seeing all the shades and hues that coloured life rather than just the ones that promised merriment – or so it had done for him and seemed to have done for Wes, as well as his brother, Richard, and his cousin, Darcy.

"So will you join us?" Wes pressed.

"I am certain we would be delighted to be a part of your group."

"A part of what group?" Alfred asked as he joined them. "My lord, it has been an age since I saw you last."

"Ah, young Alfred." Wes stood and extended his hand in greeting. "I was just inviting you and your cousin to join us at the theatre tomorrow." He motioned for Alfred to take a seat. "I also understand you are in need of a living and a wife."

Alfred scowled at Lorcan. "My mother thinks I am," he grumbled. "And so, it seems, does my companion."

"Guardian." The right side of Lorcan's mouth tipped into a teasing smirk.

"Am I missing something?" Wes asked.

"My mother would not let me come to town unaccompanied."

Wes chuckled. "Well, at the risk of sounding like an ancient curmudgeon, Lori has connections which could prove valuable to you in both securing a living and a wife, and you do not."

Alfred sighed and rolled his eyes. "I am aware of that. However, I should have liked to have asked him to help me rather than have his rather unwilling assistance forced on me."

"Your mother's insistence was necessary," Lorcan replied. He would not have willingly subjected himself to accompanying his cousin to town. He would have most soundly refused had it not been for his aunt and mother conspiring to see him sent back to town.

His head tipped as a thought struck him. "Alfred?"

"Yes."

"Was it your mother's idea for you to come to town in search of a situation or was it my mother's?"

He shrugged. "I assume it was my mother's, but the idea was presented after our mothers had spent an afternoon together. Do you suspect it was really your mother wishing to be rid of you?"

Lorcan cocked an eyebrow at Wes. "No, I suspect it was someone else entirely." And, it was not so much Alfred's future that had initiated the notion for him and Lorcan to return to town as it was Lorcan's future.

"My mother?" Wes asked in surprise.

"She does like to get her way."

"I will not deny that."

Alfred looked between them in confusion.

"Has there been any gossip?" Lorcan asked.

"You mean about you and –"

"Yes," Lorcan interrupted his friend.

"None that I have heard."

"Then, perhaps the idea did not originate with your mother." He rubbed the back of his neck. If there had been damaging gossip, he would have expected Lady Matlock to send for him directly, and surely, she knew that Kitty was not in town – "It was her. It had to be."

"How do you know?"

"Why would she want you to return to town?" Alfred inserted.

"Because she wanted me to offer for," he darted a look around the room, "Miss Bennet after – well, you know since Mr. Bingley has informed you of that particular incident."

"Ah," Alfred nodded as if everything was perfectly clear to him, and likely, it was. He was rather good at piecing things together with the barest of facts. Or perhaps, it was a ruse, for he rarely admitted to knowing the details of a situation until it was obvious to nearly all.

"How do you know it was Mother?" Wes repeated.

"I assume Lady Matlock knew that Miss Bennet had been invited to return to town?"

Wes chuckled and shook his head. "Lydia," he muttered.

"I beg your pardon?" Alfred said.

Yes, Lorcan thought, perhaps it was a ruse, and his cousin was just as confused now as he was.

"Do not tell my mother that I was the source of this information." Lord Westonbury skewered both Lorcan and Alfred with a severe look.

Lorcan raised his right hand. "On my honour."

"Mine, too," Alfred agreed.

"Lydia said she had written to her father, begging for Kitty to be able to return to town, and my mother was delighted with the idea. She thought it would be lovely if the Bingleys could come to town for a week or so before retiring to the country with the Darcys." He shrugged. "My mother is absolutely delighted to have Lydia as a future daughter. They seem to share an affinity for scheming."

"So it would seem," Lorcan muttered while Alfred chuckled.

"Do you suppose she paid your coachman to tamper with the carriage wheel?" Alfred asked.

"I would not fade away in a dead faint from surprise if it was revealed she had," Lorcan replied.

Wes chuckled. "I doubt my mother is that devious."

Lorcan was not so certain and allowed his

expression to show his doubt of Wes's words. "She refused to allow you to enter Matlock House when Miss Mary arrived, and then, once you were ill, she refused to allow you to leave. She even dismissed your servants."

"Very well," Wes said, "she might be that devious, but I still doubt she was the reason your carriage wheel suffered a break so close to Netherfield." He placed both hands on the arm of his chair and pushed up. "I will say, however, that she was partially behind my finding you here today, which means you must return to Matlock House with me for a cup of tea." He looked expectantly at Lorcan who had remained seated although Alfred had risen. "Do you truly wish to refuse her invitation? It will give you a chance to introduce your cousin to my father."

Lorcan blew out a breath and rose to join Westonbury and Alfred in going to Matlock House for tea. "I suppose we can join you," he said as if he had ever really had any choice in the matter.

Chapter 9

Mary,

When you are sharing all that Jane has written with our sisters, would you be so kind as to share my eager anticipation of Georgiana's arrival with her? There is so much I wish to discuss with her. Also, tell her that I have promised myself to practice our duet most faithfully until her arrival.

Give my love to my sisters. It will be lovely for us all to be together again.

Kitty

Georgiana smiled as she read the short note at the bottom of the letter which Mary had just finished reading.

Kitty was playing their duet again. That was a step forward.

The two letters Georgiana had received over the past month had both contained apologies from

Kitty about not being able to practice that particular piece of music as it was the one she and Georgiana had feigned a need to practice on that dreadful day when instead of receiving a declaration of love, the bright and happy future of her dear friend and new sister had begun to crumble.

"I found him." Georgiana's cousin, Lord Westonbury stepped into the drawing room at Matlock House where all of the Bennet ladies, who were in town, as well as their gentlemen, and Lord and Lady Matlock were gathered. Mr. Langley and another fellow stood behind Wes.

"This is Langley's cousin, Mr. Alfred Langley. Young Alfred–"

Georgiana nearly giggled both at the appellation her cousin used for Mr. Langley's cousin and the way a scowl briefly touched that gentleman's handsome face.

"–may I present my mother and father, Mrs. Darcy, Mr. Darcy, Miss Darcy, Miss Lydia Bennet – my brother whom you already know – and the prettiest lady in the room, Lady Westonbury."

"Honestly, Reginald, you should learn to present people properly," Lady Matlock scolded, though she did not truly look offended at how informally her eldest son had conducted introductions.

"Young Alfred is Lori's cousin. We are nearly family." Wes motioned for Mr. Langley and his cousin to find a seat while he made his way to Mary's side and gave her cheek a kiss.

"I do not see how." Lady Matlock shared a secret smile with Lydia.

"Langley and I have known each other long enough to be related," Wes replied. "I count him as dear as a brother or cousin."

"Supposing one to be related does not make it so," Lady Matlock argued. "However, I will allow that we are on familiar enough terms with Mr. Langley to not stand too firmly on protocol."

"Thank you, my lady," Mr. Langley replied before Wes could say anything. "I count it an honor."

He looked rather uneasy.

"We are happy to have you returned to us," Lady Matlock assured him. "I understand," she continued, "from Mrs. Bingley's letter, that you were fortunate enough to have stayed at Netherfield. I trust you found everyone in good health and happiness?"

His look of unease seemed to deepen. "Yes," he answered simply.

"Mrs. Bingley was well?" Lady Matlock pressed.

"She was, as was her husband."

"And Miss Bennet?"

"She and her sister were busy making preparations for a soiree." Mr. Langley held Lady Matlock's gaze while not entirely answering the question that had been asked.

"She has promised to practice our duet," Georgiana inserted since sitting by and allowing her aunt to poke and prod at Mr. Langley made her nearly as uncomfortable as Mr. Langley looked. "One cannot practice a difficult piece of music if one is unwell."

"I will give you that, and I know planning a soiree is best done when one is well and not overset with anything," her aunt agreed. She turned back to Mr. Langley. "And your family is well?"

"Yes, my lady."

"And yours Mr. Alfred Langley?"

"There was not so much as a sniffle or cough when I last saw them, my lady."

Mr. Alfred Langley seemed a very relaxed sort of person.

"That is excellent news. Are you in town on business or for the festivities of the season?"

"Young Alfred needs a wife," Wes said with a smirk.

"No, Young Alfred does not need a wife," Mr. Alfred Langley retorted. "Young Alfred's mother thinks he does, but he does not."

"Oh, every gentleman needs a wife," Lord Matlock countered. "Just ask my wife, she will assure you it is true."

A ripple of laughter spread around the room.

"It is true," Lady Matlock said. "And I am not opposed to helping you find one."

"I am grateful to you for your offer. However, I think it is best to be established in a good situation before seriously pursuing a wife. I am currently without a place to practice my profession, and that would be a very untenable situation into which to bring a wife – even an heiress as my mother suggests I should find." He shook his head. "I fully intend to put my education to some sort of use no matter what sort of wealth a lady might bring with her as my wife."

"So, you are not a fortune hunter?" Lady Matlock asked.

He shook his head. "I will not say that a lady with some funds would not make life easier, but I intend to find a companion when I finally am established."

Georgiana had to keep her mouth from dropping open at such a forward admission by a gentleman. She had never heard any of the few gentlemen she knew, who were not related to her, speak so candidly about marriage, professions, and money. It would make things a lot easier for a lady if they did.

"That begs the question," Richard said, "what is your profession?"

"I am bound to the church," Alfred answered. "I have just completed a time of being a curate to a very fine parson. However, a curacy is not sufficient to see to the care of myself and a family." He shrugged. "I have been thinking about marrying, not that I have admitted such to my mother."

"Do you have a lady in mind?"

"My lady," Lord Matlock rumbled softly.

"I do not mind the inquiry," Alfred assured him. "No, there is no particular lady. I have only been considering the needs of a family and positioning myself so that I am best able to meet them before I set out on my search."

"A search will be much harder once you have a living," Mr. Langley cautioned. "You cannot just leave your parish to attend the season."

"Unless I have a curate," Alfred replied with a smile. "However, town is not the only place to find a wife."

"Indeed, it is not," Lord Matlock agreed. He tipped his head and studied Alfred for a moment. "I have a living that will be falling open soon. The current parson is just beginning to ail as a result of age – he is becoming very arthritic – and his daughter and her husband are wanting to have him join them so that they can see to his care. Do you have any letters of recommendation?"

Was this then how parsons were given positions? Were not such positions given just because a gentleman wished to favour the son of a friend as her father had attempted to do?

"You have no one who is expecting the living?" Alfred countered. "Such a thing could be valuable when seeking support for a vote."

Ah! So, there were those who gave livings as some sort of reward for a connection. It was not just her father. She exhaled. That made her feel better.

Lord Matlock chuckled. "You are astute. No doubt, I could find someone to fill the position and bolster my own situation. However, this parish is dear to me, and I would not wish to have the parishioners, which includes myself, left to just anyone's care."

"Then," Alfred replied, "I shall send around copies of my letters of recommendation at the beginning of the week if that meets with your approval, my lord."

"It does, and I am going to ask you to call on my wife and me several times so that I might observe you and gain a better acquaintance."

"He and Lori are to join us at the theater tomorrow," Wes inserted.

"Are they?" Lady Matlock looked thoroughly delighted.

The conversation fell into a natural discussion of plays and such while the tea service was made ready. Then, with cups of tea distributed and a tray of sweets and sandwiches adequately relieved of its contents, the occupants of the room moved about and had smaller, quieter conversations. Mr. Alfred

Langley ended up standing at the window with her uncle, most likely discussing whatever gentlemen might discuss about churches in need of parsons.

Her aunt and Lydia were also intently discussing something while Richard sat in a chair with his eyes closed listening to what was happening in the room. Next to him was where Georgiana decided to enjoy her cup of tea.

"Is that duet *the* duet?" he asked, peeking one eye open to look at her briefly before closing it again.

"Yes," she whispered. "She and Mr. Langley must have spoken and reached some sort of understanding." Or so she hoped.

Richard was the only one who knew both that Kitty had stopped practicing that piece of music and the reason why. He was also the one who had assured her that Mr. Langley was not the sort to toy with a lady's heart and that he suspected Mr. Langley was lying about not wishing to marry Kitty. He had always been the easier of her two guardians to whom to speak about such things – even when he did get angry, it did not cut her heart the way it did when her brother looked disappointed, for Fitzwilliam reminded her so much of her dearly loved father.

He peeked his eye open once again. "Wes and Langley are discussing Netherfield." Then, he closed his eye again and motioned for her to be silent.

Georgiana studied the floral pattern on her cup and concentrated on listening to her cousin and his friend who were just a short distance away from them.

"Your offer was not rejected out of hand?" Wes asked.

An offer had been made? Georgiana peeked at Mr. Langley who was not looking pleased.

"Could we not talk about this elsewhere?"

"There is nowhere else. Everyone is occupied, and even if someone hears, they will not carry tales."

Mr. Langley huffed. "Very well. Yes, it was rejected but not out of hand."

Georgiana lifted her cup to her lips. Kitty had rejected him again? Why was she so insistent that she was not ready to marry? If Georgiana had a gentleman like Mr. Langley, who, though he had appeared for a time to look as if he was inconstant or roguish, now appeared to be quite devoted, she would not hesitate to give him her heart and her promise.

"Does she love you?"

"Yes."

The right side of Georgiana's lips tipped up into a half-smile. Kitty had been completely smitten with Mr. Langley. That was why his rejection had crushed her so. It was good to hear that her heart had not been completely destroyed in the process and that her friend was still able to love Mr. Langley. Of course, that did not explain why Kitty would reject him again.

Try as she might, Georgiana had not been able to get Kitty to reveal her true reason for the rejection other than she was not ready to be a wife, for she was far too young. However, from the way she had been unable to look Georgiana in the eye when saying such, Georgiana knew that there was another reason for her refusal.

"Did she give you a reason?"

Bless her cousin for being the curious and persistent sort.

"She said there was no hurry."

Again, as she lifted her cup for a sip of tea, Georgiana dared to peek at Mr. Langley, who was shaking his head as if bewildered.

"There is some promise that prevents her from accepting me."

Georgiana's cup stopped just at her lips and lowered again without being relieved of a single drop of tea. No, it couldn't be, could it?

"A promise to whom?" Wes asked.

"I do not know other than it is a friend."

Oh, dear. It was her. She was the reason her friend had suffered heartbreak. No wonder Kitty would not look at her when she spoke of her rejection or tell her the truth. She lifted her cup to her lips once more and this time took several sips.

This would not do. This simply would not do.

Chapter 10

Kitty had only taken two steps into Netherfield's library before turning around and darting out of the room. She stood near the partially open door and listened for the sound of voices to indicate that entering might be safe. She placed her hands, which were cool, on her cheeks to keep them from growing any warmer than they were.

"What are you doing? Are you eavesdropping?" Lydia whispered as she came to stand next to Kitty.

"Yes," Kitty replied.

"Have you heard anything of interest?" Lydia leaned toward the door to the library. Her brow furrowed. "I do not hear anything. Is there someone in there?"

"Mary and Lord Westonbury," Kitty replied.

Lydia's eyes grew wide. "Were they..." She did

not finish the question with any words but rather, she finished it with a circular wave of her hand.

Kitty had no idea what that motion meant. "They were kissing." She looked up and down the corridor. "Most passionately. His hands – well, they are married so he is allowed, but I would rather not watch them even if I do want a book."

Lydia giggled. "Can you believe that is Mary?"

Kitty shook her head. She absolutely could not believe their most proper sister was allowing a gentleman to do that to her – even if that gentleman was her husband and a former rake.

"It is dreadful how often I have witnessed something similar. Mama would be shocked."

Kitty could understand that. She, herself, was shocked. "They are always so amorous?"

Lydia nodded. "Often. It is best to make some sort of noise before entering an unoccupied room when they are visiting." She grabbed Kitty by the arm and pulled her down the corridor. "We will pretend we have heard the most humorous story ever. Do not laugh quietly."

Lydia turned Kitty back in the direction of the library and began laughing. "And then, you will never believe what she said next." She nudged Kitty. "Ask me what she said next," she hissed.

"What did she say?"

"You must not tell anyone." Lydia cupped a hand around her mouth as she spoke into Kitty's ear. "Pretend to be shocked and then burst into laughter. It will give them time to be proper when we enter the room."

Lydia was the best at scheming and so, Kitty complied.

"No!" she cried. "She did not!"

"I swear she did."

"Oh, my!" Kitty said before beginning to laugh.

"Compose yourself when you see them," Lydia whispered between giggles. She covered her mouth and slowly stopped giggling as she entered the library arm in arm with Kitty. "Oh!"

She was excellent at pretending almost any emotion such as the surprise she was feigning now. Kitty was only marginally as good as Lydia, but she hoped it was enough to appear unflustered by the way Mary was fidgeting with the lace at her neckline.

"Kitty wished for a book." Lydia appeared a trifle amused but other than that, she seemed as normal as ever – not at all like a person who had just inter-rupted an amorous exchange between her sister and that sister's husband.

"You may join us," Lord Westonbury offered.

"I do not think that is wise," Lydia said with a smirk.

"And why is that not wise?" Lord Westonbury replied.

"No reason," Lydia fibbed. "I just do not think it is wise is all."

"That is not an acceptable answer," Lord West-onbury retorted.

"Do you think it is wise for us to join you, Mary?" Lydia asked with a bat of her lashes.

Mary blushed and looked down. "I do not see why it would be a horrid idea."

"I have found it," Kitty grabbed a book from the shelf in front of which she stood. It was poetry. That would do. She just needed something to read before bed and when all her other sisters were occupied with their gentlemen as she knew they would be. It really did not matter what kind of poems the book contained so long as they gave her somewhere to be where she would not feel so alone.

"Has Darcy arrived?" Lord Westonbury asked before Kitty could scoot away.

"No, not yet, my lord," she answered.

"Wes," he said. "Call me Wes. My lord is so formal. We are family after all."

"Thank you, my – Wes." She grimaced and shook her head. "It feels wrong."

Wes laughed. "You will get used to it. I plan to call you Kitty." Again, he laughed when her eyes grew wide. "You will also get used to that."

"If you say so, my – If you say so." Kitty was not entirely certain she would get used to it. He was a viscount after all.

"We have not yet had an opportunity to talk since I arrived two hours ago." Wes motioned to a chair across from where he and Mary sat.

Kitty clutched her book to her chest and sat down as he has requested — but only on the edge of the chair. He tipped his head and studied her.

"You may relax. I promise to be kind," he whispered. "My wife will not allow me to be anything else. She is a fierce one. Has she ever scolded you?" There was a teasing note to his words that caused Kitty to giggle.

"She has."

"Oh, Mary scolds everyone – or she did," Lydia corrected. She had not taken a seat and seemed uncertain if she should stay or leave.

Wes looked at Lydia and nodded toward the door. "Tell him we are in here."

With a word of thanks, Lydia scooted out the door.

Had Lydia been on her way to see Colonel Fitzwilliam and stopped to help her? Kitty shook her head and smiled. The changes in her younger sister continued to amaze Kitty.

"She is quite different, isn't she?" Mary's question was quiet.

Kitty nodded. "But then, so are you."

Mary smiled. "I like to think of it as having found my best self." She smiled at Wes. "I think that is what love does, it compels you to better yourself but not for yourself – for the person you love." She turned back to Kitty. "And not because he demands it." She shook her head. "Because your heart demands it."

"I know it has changed me," Wes said, lifting Mary's hand to kiss it. "Have I told you how wise my wife is?"

Kitty shook her head.

"I have not? Then, you will have to ask your cousins, for I have told them many times."

Kitty blinked. "My cousins?"

Wes nodded. "Clarissa, Albert, Hugh, and John. I have told them each time we have had tea together."

"You have had tea with my cousins?"

Wes shrugged. "They are my cousins as well now."

"He insists upon a weekly visit," Mary said. "Wes is rather taken with them."

"They are delightful, and I think it is good practice for being a father someday." He smirked. "A lord learns you know."

Mary rolled her eyes which was in stark contrast to the smile she wore. Kitty sighed.

"Is something wrong?" Mary asked.

Kitty shook her head. "You are just so obviously happy."

"You could be as well," Wes said in a quiet and serious tone which caused Kitty's heart to flutter uneasily. "You just need to accept the right fellow."

Kitty breathed a sigh of relief. She was afraid he was going to begin speaking about his friend. Jane knew that she and Lorcan had parted on good terms, but she had not even told Lydia that yet. There had not been a moment to speak privately with Lydia since her arrival. Her sister had been occupied with making certain Colonel Fitzwilliam was well, and then assuring herself that Jane was not putting too much stress and strain on herself and her baby.

"We saw Mr. Langley in town," Mary added. "He and his cousin joined us for tea on three occasions and attended the theater with us once."

"They were also at a musicale we attended," Wes added.

Kitty ran the ribbon on her dress – her green dress which went so well with the ribbon Lorcan had rescued from Oliver — through her fingers. It appeared they were going to talk about Lord Westonbury's friend. "Was he well?" she asked without lifting her eyes.

"He was, though he seemed to be wishing time away," Wes replied.

"What do you mean?"

"I dare say he will be much better than well in about three days' time when he gets to see you."

"Oh," Kitty's face was instantly hot.

"Are you glad to be returning to town?" Mary said when the room remained silent.

"Yes, very. I have missed Georgiana."

"Only Georgiana?" Wes questioned.

Kitty blew out a breath. "Until recently, yes."

"You did not miss Lori?"

"Wes," Mary scolded.

Kitty swallowed and shook her head. "I regretted him – which is a far more grievous emotion than missing someone."

Lord Westonbury smiled. "I will take that as hopeful news on the behalf of my friend then."

"You are not angry with me? For refusing your friend?" She had feared that Lord Westonbury – Wes – would be put out with her for her refusal of his friend and quite happy that his friend had disentangled himself from her. There were many things she had supposed that seemed to have been wrong.

"I was shocked and dismayed, of course," Wes answered very honestly, "but I was not angry – at least, not with you. Lori, on the other hand, was called a few choice words when I discovered he had not made a formal offer to you." His lips pressed into a thin line as he shook his head. "No man should deny his heart like that."

"He thought he was doing what I wanted," Kitty said quickly. She simply could not allow anyone to think ill of Lorcan when he was attempting to be so noble.

"I understand his reasons now. However, I do not know yours."

"Wes, it is not our affair to know," Mary scolded.

"Am I to believe that you do not wish to know Kitty's reasons for refusing Lori and then regretting him?"

"I did not say that," Mary replied. "Regardless of my curiosity, it is not for me to know unless Kitty wishes to tell me."

"And how will she know you wish to know if you do not ask?" Wes said.

"I cannot tell you," Kitty inserted. "Please, do not argue because of me."

Mary smiled at her. "We are not arguing. Not yet."

"Are you not?" It certainly sounded as if they were.

"We are debating. And my husband has a good point, as he often does. However, I was not going to ask so soon or so directly." She smiled sheepishly.

"I cannot tell you," Kitty said as a Dash came into the room with his nose nearly pressed to the floor while he sniffed a trail that stopped at Kitty's feet.

He sat and looked at her with his tongue hanging out of his mouth and his tail thumping the floor happily, waiting for Kitty to scratch his ear.

"I take it Darcy has arrived," Wes said.

"You found her! Good boy!" Georgiana cried as she entered the room followed by her brother and Elizabeth. "I told him we were going to find Kitty, and he has been so eager to arrive – nearly so eager as I was." She threw her arms around Kitty. "I have something I wish to tell you," she whispered near Kitty's ear.

"And I have something I wish to tell you," Kitty replied. "Oh! I am so glad you are here. I have missed you so dearly."

"And I, you," Georgiana replied.

"Have you been shown to a room yet?"

"No, Dash and I had to find you first." Georgiana hugged Kitty again. "A month is a very long time."

"May I get a hug?" Wes asked.

Georgiana giggled. "I saw you yesterday."

"But it has been a whole day. Do not tell me you have not missed me at least a trifle."

Georgiana threw her arms around her cousin. "I cannot say I have thought of you even once since seeing you yesterday as I have been completely consumed with my eagerness to see Kitty again. However, I am happy to see you." She turned to Mary. "And you as well."

"You must also hug my wife, or I shall have to do it for you."

"No!" both Kitty and Georgiana cried.

"At least, not until we leave the room," Georgiana added with a laugh before embracing Mary. "Your travels were good?"

"Very," Wes said with a wide grin.

"Westonbury," Darcy grumbled.

"The roads were good, and the sky was clear. Our travels were very good. I do not know why you took exception to my reply."

His words might proclaim his innocence, but to Kitty, he did not look at all innocent, though she was not entirely certain why Mr. Darcy was grumbling at him.

"Come, Kitty. You must help me settle into my room."

"Not without a hug for me," Elizabeth said, wrapping Kitty in her arms. "I am so happy to see you. Are you well?"

"Yes, I am."

"And your heart, is it also well?"

Kitty nodded.

Elizabeth hugged her once again. "I am happy to hear it. Now, before Georgiana bursts with excitement, you must go see her to her room."

And that is exactly what Kitty did, with Dash trailing behind.

Chapter 11

Georgiana opened the small bag in which all the things she needed for her dressing table were located. Whenever she travelled, her maid saw to her gowns and such, but this bag, this one, was always Georgiana's to unpack. That was how it had always been. There was something about arranging the things she would use at this table which just made her feel as if she were at home whether it was in a guest room or one of her own bedchambers.

Dash, who had followed Georgiana and Kitty to Georgiana's room, growled from his place of repose midway between the bed and the dressing table.

Georgiana glanced over her shoulder. "Oliver is a friend."

Oliver was slinking along the edge of the room.

"He is a ribbon thief," Kitty said from her perch on the bed.

"Are you, indeed, Mr. Oliver?" Georgiana directed the question at the grey tabby who was now sitting very prettily and licking a paw.

"He most certainly is! If it had not been for Mr. Langley coming to its rescue, one of my ribbons would have been lost to me because Oliver stole it."

Georgiana wished to hug Oliver for his pilfering for it had brought her just the opening for which she had been wishing. Since the day he and his cousin had first come to tea at Matlock House, she had wanted to speak to Kitty about Mr. Langley, and, for a day and a half now as she had prepared to travel to Netherfield, she had been attempting to figure out the best way to broach the subject. She was certain, from what she had heard, that her friend was in love with the gentleman and would not dissolve into tears at the mention of his name, but there was that small voice of worry which caused her to doubt herself.

"I saw Mr. Langley recently. He came to tea at Matlock House when I was there one day. I believe it was not long after he had been here."

"Was his cousin with him?"

Kitty's eagerness to hear about the Langley gentleman caused Georgiana to smile and her worry to dissolve.

"Yes, he was," she answered. "I think my uncle might give him one of the livings under his purview."

"Oh, that is excellent news!"

"He seemed pleased with the notion." Georgiana placed her jewelry box on the dressing table at the top on the righthand side. There were only her brush and a bottle of fragrance to place before her task would be complete. "As did his cousin."

"I have something I must tell you."

From the way Kitty was winding the ribbon on her dress through her fingers, what she had to tell Georgiana made her uncomfortable. For all the boisterous and self-assured behaviour Georgiana had witness upon first meeting Kitty and her sisters, the real Kitty, or the Kitty whom Georgiana now knew and claimed as her dearest friend, was anything but those things. But then, it seemed Kitty's sisters – Mary and Lydia that is – were not as they had first appeared either.

Georgiana chided herself about needing to learn how to decipher character better. She had been attempting to learn to do so ever since Ramsgate, but it appeared she still had a bit of work to do.

"What did you wish to tell me?"

"It is about Mr. Langley." Kitty glanced up from watching her fingers play with her ribbon. "He loves me."

Georgiana took her time placing her bottle of fragrance on her table and making certain that each item was in its place as she waited for Kitty to continue.

"Are you not surprised?"

Georgiana shook her head.

"Why ever not? We both thought he had played with my heart."

Georgiana turned toward her friend. A little flutter of anxiety flitted through her breast. "I overheard him talking to Wes." She crossed to sit next to her friend. "That is what I wished to speak to you about because something I heard troubled me."

"What did you hear?" Kitty's eyes were large with concern. "He did not lie to me about loving me, did he?"

Georgiana grasped Kitty's hands. "No, I am certain he loves you since he has offered for you–"

"You know about that?" Kitty asked in surprise.

"It was part of what I overheard. He seems most anxious for you to accept him. Your hesitance to do so is where the troublesome bit lies."

"I do not understand."

"Kitty, dearest Kitty," Georgiana said as she squeezed her friend's hands, "do not let me keep you from accepting him. I cannot hold you to a promise that would see you unhappy for one moment longer." She swallowed and blinked against the emotions that wished to spill out. "I am so sorry to have been the cause of your pain. Can you forgive me?"

"There is nothing to forgive!" Kitty cried. "You did not cause my sorrow. Mr. Langley did, but not because he wished to hurt me," she added hastily. "He was trying to do what he thought I wanted."

"But if you had never made that promise to me about helping me through my first season, you would have accepted him in the music room at Matlock House. It is my fear of choosing wrongly which has brought you pain; therefore, I was the cause."

Kitty's lips were set in an obstinate line as she shook her head. "No, you were not."

"But your promise – the one which keeps you from accepting Mr. Langley – was to me." If she had known that Kitty's promise was the reason she had refused Mr. Langley all those weeks ago, she would have declared the promise null and void then – which, she supposed, was the reason Kitty would not tell her. Kitty was a kind and loyal friend, but at present, both her kindness and loyalty were a step too far in Georgiana's opinion.

"I chose to make the promise," Kitty continued. "You did not force it on me. Indeed, you did not ask me to make it. I offered it, and I will not let you claim responsibility for any trouble which has arisen because of it."

Georgiana sighed. She knew that, along with being kind and loyal to a fault, her friend was also stubborn at times. "Very well. I will attempt not to feel an ounce of guilt for your having endured over a month of regret and sorrow. In return, however, I would ask that you forget your promise, as I absolve you of it, and accept Mr. Langley."

"Are you no longer fearful then?"

She was. She really, really was. However, Georgiana could not admit to that. Not now when she needed Kitty to agree to accept Mr. Langley.

"Do you know who is or is not trustworthy?" Kitty did not look as if she was prepared to believe a positive answer to either of her questions.

"I am certain I can figure it out. I shall just watch to see how my brother responds to all the gentlemen who come to call, and then, I shall ask Elizabeth if I am still uncertain."

"Are you certain that would work?"

Georgiana nodded.

"Then, you do not need me?"

The hurt in Kitty's tone cut Georgiana's heart.

"Of course, I need you. I have no other dearer friend."

"Then, allow me to help you," Kitty begged.

"You must know, surely, you must know that I will still wish for your guidance," Georgiana assured. "I only want you to know that I will not be left to the wolves by your marrying Mr. Langley."

Kitty pulled her bottom lip between her teeth, her eyes seemed fixed on something to her left, but Georgiana knew she was not actually looking at anything in particular. This was the expression Kitty wore when she contemplated things of great importance. Silently, Georgiana waited to hear her friend's response.

"Lorcan –"

Georgiana smiled at her friend's familiar reference to Mr. Langley.

"– suggested we enter a betrothal, knowing that a wedding would not happen until after my promise was complete. Not that he knows what the promise is," Kitty hastened to assure Georgiana, who already knew that from what she had heard at Matlock House.

"And you did not accept such a generous offer?" It was neither a perfect arrangement nor the one for which Georgiana wished, but it seemed a most unselfish compromise for Mr. Langley to make.

"I was not certain if that would break my promise or not."

"I do not see how it would break your promise." It would, however, delay her friend's happiness by a year.

"I did not either when he suggested it, but I needed to be certain." Kitty looked painfully perplexed about something.

"Are you certain you wish to wait so long?" Georgiana asked gently. She would still attempt to reason with Kitty, but she did not wish to add to whatever it was which was troubling her.

"It is not so very long."

To Georgiana, Kitty's tone seemed to say that it was long. Maybe that was what was causing her friend's unease. "You are a dear friend to be willing to put your happiness to the side on my behalf, but are you adamant that I cannot convince you to forget about your promise altogether?"

"Yes. I should very much like to stand by your side at soirees and whisper, behind closed doors, about the gentlemen we meet." The furrow left Kitty's brow, and her features seemed to sigh with relief.

"We could still do that if you were married." Georgiana had to try again to persuade her friend to seek her own happiness.

"It would not be the same," Kitty protested, the furrow once again appearing in her brow. "We would not be able to sit like this in your room for hours at a time or in our night clothes as we discussed each soiree and every gentleman. I would not get to help you choose your dresses, and you would not be able to help me pick the best accompaniments to my gowns."

"I think we could have a portion of that, and you could still have your own happiness."

Kitty shook her head. "What sort of friend or sister would I be if I put my desires above yours?"

"Then my desire is to see you married before I step one foot into a ballroom for my first season."

"You are just saying that. I will not be moved."

Georgiana scowled. "You should be moved. I shall feel dreadful keeping you from your future."

"You are not allowed to feel dreadful," Kitty protested. "*This* is my future. Helping you, while being betrothed to Lorcan, is my very happy future." She smiled. "He is coming to call on me to hear my answer as soon as I have returned to town." She drew and released a deep breath. "I am so glad to know what I shall tell him."

"I still wish you were telling him something different," Georgiana said softly.

"I am happy," Kitty said. "This arrangement will give me a great deal of time to prepare for my marriage and to learn more about my future husband all while doing my duty to a friend and sister. Please, be happy for me."

"If you are happy, then so am I," Georgiana assured her. "However, might I suggest one small amendment to your promise?"

Kitty's left brow arched in question.

"I propose that your promise to me has been fulfilled either at the end of my season or, if it should happen before the end of the season, when I find a gentleman of good character to court me. There would be no reason for you to need to help me discern character if I have already found an acceptable gentleman, would there be?"

"I suppose there would not be."

"Then, we are agreed?"

Kitty nodded her head, though seemingly with some reluctance. "Yes, we are agreed."

Georgiana threw her arms around her friend. "Then, I am excessively happy for you." And just as determined to find someone to court as soon as could be managed.

Chapter 12

The clock at the top of the stairs chimed twice. On the bedside table, Lorcan's nearly spent candle flickered and sputtered while he rose from the chair where he had been sitting with an open, and completely ignored, book on his knee for the better part of an hour. As he removed his robe and slippers, he wondered if Kitty was as anxious about seeing him as he was about calling on her.

He climbed into bed. Maybe this time when he laid down, he would actually fall asleep. He opened the door on the lantern which held his candle and, with a quick exhale, extinguished the flame.

Tomorrow, he would have his answer, and with any luck, he would be a blissfully betrothed gentleman before dinner. Though he hoped that he would not have to wait to marry her, Lorcan knew that the likelihood of marrying soon was nothing more than a fantasy. He would like to think that, should Kitty accept his offer, he would happily wait for her to be his wife because all he needed to know was that she loved him. However, the truth was that he was impatient. He wanted to marry her now, not later, and it wasn't because his body cried out for her – though it did. No, his impatience came down to the fact that, since the moment he had danced that first set of dances with her — the one which he had claimed to spite Westonbury — he had known that the part of him which had always been restless and seeking was satiated by her. As he had pondered that fact over the past few days, he had come to realize that she stirred something so great within him that to call it love seemed too feeble a word.

He rolled to his side and bunched the pillow under his head. He desired her as he had never desired anything else in his life. He wanted her in his bed. He would not lie about that. The mere thought of her lying here with him... He blew out a slow breath and willed himself to remain relaxed. Not even the touch of a practiced courtesan had affected him as just the thought of Kitty did – but then, he had not loved Clarice, and Clarice had not loved him. It had been an exercise in self-gratification, nothing more. But Kitty? Kitty was more. So very much more.

And that was why, though he was impatient to take her as his wife, he would willingly, if not happily, wait for her to do whatever it was she needed to do before she married him because taking Kitty as his wife was not just about taking her to bed and finding pleasure in her body. It was about finding the part of him which seemed to be missing and cherishing her for eternity. Love, that altogether inadequate descriptor for how he felt about Kitty, would provide him with the patience he needed.

He ran a hand over the empty spot on the mattress next to him, and with a whispered, "Good night, my love," to his absent companion, Lorcan closed his eyes and, after a few minutes of deliberately deep and slow breaths, drifted off into the misty shadows of the night to join Kitty in his dreams until he could call on her in the brightness of a new day.

~*~*~

"Richard," Lorcan greeted Colonel Fitzwilliam with a nod as the man entered the breakfast room where Lorcan and Alfred were indulging in a hearty meal the following morning. "Do you wish for a plate?"

"A cup of coffee and a scone would be most welcome."

Lorcan looked to the footman near the door, who inclined his head and began the task of retrieving the required pieces of silver and china which were needed.

"What brings you to visit so early?" Lorcan asked.

"A message to you from my brother and my cousin."

"Westonbury could not deliver it himself?" With his plate emptied of its meal, Lorcan took up a position of easy repose and sipped his coffee.

"To quote my brother 'you have no wife and, therefore, no reason to lie abed in the morning' which according to him, meant it would be a very small inconvenience for me to call on you in his place." Richard's lips tipped up into a smile. "And truth be told. I find it refreshing to be called on to do something for someone rather than being seen only as a recovering invalid."

"How is the sight?" Lorcan asked.

"No better, and no worse. I'd not wish it on anyone, but it is becoming normal."

"What is wrong with your sight?" Alfred asked.

"I cannot see on one side. If you approach me on the left, I will have to turn my head to see you."

"Indeed? That is rather inconvenient, is it not?"

"Excessively, but Lydia takes care of the inconvenience when she is present."

"How so?" Alfred asked.

"She will direct people to stand where I can see them, or she will whisper to me when someone has approached whom I would not be able to see." He lifted his cup and took a sip. "I have come to rely on her a great deal."

"That is as it should be," Alfred said. "A wife – or, in this case, a future wife – should be a helpmate."

He knew his cousin had studied to be a parson, and he knew that Alfred had excelled in his studies, yet it still startled Lorcan to hear him voice statements that seemed more fitting of a clergyman twice Alfred's age.

"We are to be partners of sorts. Neither husband nor wife is better than the other, though the responsibility for the care and comfort of our wives and families does fall to us as gentlemen." Alfred took another sip of coffee. "That is another reason why I am in no rush to marry. It is a grave duty to be the proper head of a family." He gave Lorcan a pointed look.

"What is that look about?"

"I wanted to make certain you were listening as you will need the advice far sooner than I will," he replied.

"And Richard will need it before me."

"Yes, well, he seems to be settled into his role quite well, and having commanded a group of men, I do think he is fully familiar with grave duty."

"And I am not?"

Alfred shook his head. "Perhaps you are. Perhaps you are not."

"I am."

"Then, why did you refuse to marry Miss Bennet when the need to do so was presented to you?" Again, his younger cousin skewered him with a pointed look.

"It was not because I do not take marriage seriously if that is what you mean."

"Perhaps you do, and perhaps you do not."

Lorcan gaped at Alfred, who was looking excessively at ease and a bit amused. "Of all the infuriating cousins in this world, I had to be blessed with the most trying."

Alfred laughed. "I was shocked beyond being able to contain my surprise when Bingley told me you had refused to do the right thing by Miss Bennet." He looked at Richard. "He likes to have his fun. He is your brother's friend, after all. But when it comes to doing what he knows is right, Lori would have to have a very good reason for not doing it." He turned back to Lorcan. "And I would like to know what that reason is."

"She refused him first," Richard inserted. "And he thought by refusing to force her to marry him, he was giving her what she wanted."

"How do you know that?" Had Westonbury shared that with his brother? If so, he was going to have to have a chat with his good friend at Gentleman Jackson's.

"I did not learn it from my brother," Richard replied as if he had read Lorcan's mind. "It was Georgiana, who had it from Kitty – but you are not supposed to know that." He closed his bad eye and glared with his one good eye first at Lorcan and then Alfred. "So you can see," he said to Alfred, "he takes marriage and the desires of the lady he loves very seriously, for I dare say it cost him a great deal to put her wishes ahead of his own."

A smile split Alfred's face. "I am satisfied, and my fears that my cousin had become an utter reprobate have been alleviated. You may proceed with your message."

Lorcan shook his head. "You have overstayed your welcome," he said to Alfred.

"You cannot be rid of me until the season is over."

Richard laughed. "Actually, I have a message for you as well, Alfred. My father heard I was on my way to visit you and Lori and wished for me to give you an invitation to join him at Matlock. It seems you have made a favourable impression on him, and he would like for you to see the living and meet the parishioners."

"Does he have a wife for him as well, so that I can be truly rid of him?" Lorcan teased.

"No, but I am certain my mother and Lydia would be up for the challenge of finding one for him."

"I am not marrying yet," Alfred protested above Lorcan and Richard's laughter.

Sobering, but only slightly, Richard took a sip of his coffee. "My message for you, Lori, is, and once, again, I am quoting my brother for he insisted I deliver it word for word as he said it, 'Everyone has returned to town, and Miss Kitty seems most anxious to see you. Call on her directly, and then come to dinner in Brook Street to inform me of your happy news. Bring Young Alfred.' And my cousin Georgiana would like for me to make certain that you know that she, her brother, and Elizabeth would be delighted if Mr. Alfred Langley would join them for tea while you are driving with Kitty."

"And this could not be sent to me by way of a note?"

Richard shook his head. "I am to carry your reply to Georgie – so she can be prepared for tea, and to Lady Westonbury – so dinner can be planned appropriately."

"That could be accomplished through a note."

Richard smirked. "According to Westonbury, the mail service is so very unreliable these days. He is still not pleased that you did not inform him of your arrival in town. And as I said, I was pleased to be called on to be of service."

Lorcan should insist upon replying with a note or telling Westonbury that he had plans for the evening but would be delighted to call at Brook Street next week.

"He will hunt you down," Richard muttered.

Had the man lost part of his vision and been given the ability to read thoughts in its place?

"Then, I suppose, my answer will be that I and Young Alfred would be delighted to dine with him this evening unless, of course, my heart is in tatters. In which case, I will send Young Alfred alone."

Richard's lips tipped upward. "I very much doubt that your heart will be broken. Again, you are not supposed to know that. Now, about Georgiana's invitation and that of my father."

"Yes, to both," Alfred said.

Richard drained the last of his coffee from his cup. "Then, I guess my work here is done, and I have three other messages to deliver." He rose. "Thank you, for your hospitality, gentlemen. I will be on my way. If fortune favours me, I will be able to avail myself of another scone and a second cup of coffee when I get to Darcy's." He bowed and took his leave.

"It seems you're about to make your mother very

happy," Alfred said while Richard's footsteps still could be heard in the hall.

Lorcan cocked an eyebrow and smirked. Hopefulness welled within him making him feel decidedly light. "If only we could make your mother so happy," he teased.

"I will have a living and one which is not too far from her and father. She will have to be pleased with that." He rose to leave the room.

"Wear your most fetching coat," Lorcan said. "Remember, Miss Darcy is an heiress."

"I am not marrying yet," Alfred threw the comment over his shoulder as he left the room.

Neither was he, but if what Richard had said was right, Lorcan would soon be promised to the woman he loved.

Chapter 13

"You look lovely," Georgiana said upon entering Kitty's room at Darcy House. "Is this the dress you wore the first day you went driving with Mr. Langley?"

"It is. Do you think it is foolish for me to wish to wear it? I had thought it might be better to begin again in a completely new dress, but he said he remembered this one when he helped me get my ribbon back from Oliver that day." It had been her favourite dress since that day.

She straightened a sleeve that did not need straightening. Her stomach was all aflutter, and her heart would not remain calm. Today, she would promise herself to a gentleman whom she loved – if he was still willing to wait for her. She turned to examine her hair in the mirror. "He said he likes green and that it was a becoming colour on me."

Georgiana grasped Kitty's shoulders from behind and rested her head on one of them so that she was looking into the mirror with and at Kitty.

"It is not foolish," she said with a small laugh. "I cannot believe that my friend will soon be betrothed."

"I cannot either." She would not need to pinch her cheeks for colour today, for she expected they would be permanently flushed with joy and excitement from now until ... well, she could not imagine when actually. "Is a lady allowed to be this happy?" She turned to look at Georgiana.

"I should think so! If you were not happy at the prospect of marrying Mr. Langley, I would lock you in your room and send him away. For, no friend of mine shall be miserable."

"Do not say it," Kitty cautioned. "I do not wish to argue with you at present." Georgiana had attempted several times over the past day and a half to persuade Kitty that she did not have to keep her promise. "I will not abandon you, and I shall be excessively happy."

"You will, at least, tell him that your promise is to me and that it is only for this season or until I find a gentleman to court me?"

"Yes, I will tell him all that. I promise." Kitty blew out a breath. "Are you ready?"

Georgiana laughed. "It is not me who is expecting a suitor. I am only expecting guests, and I will not even be the hostess. There really is not much about which I need to be anxious, although, I must say, Mr. Alfred Langley is handsome." She stood with her hand on the doorknob. "I do hope he will be able to participate in a portion of the season. Do you think that unwed parsons are given time to do so?"

"Do you like him?"

"I do not know," Georgiana said with a shrug. "But I did find the answers he gave my uncle to be interesting. He seems to be a trustworthy gentleman, and I have only a few months left until I am officially out. Therefore, I thought it a good idea to start considering any gentleman I might meet now as practice for when the festivities of the season begin." Georgiana pulled her closer and lowered her voice as they walked arm and arm down the grand staircase. "A lady practices dancing and playing the piano to prepare for her come-out. Does it not make sense to practice reading characters and deciding what a lady wishes for in a husband?"

Kitty shrugged. "It sounds reasonable, I suppose."

"Then, I will begin my lessons with Mr. Alfred Langley, if you approve of him, that is."

Kitty's already anxious heart jumped to her throat. Saying one was going to help guide a friend and actually doing it were very different things. "I cannot think of a reason why he is not acceptable other than he is somewhat of an annoyance to his cousin at times."

"So are Richard and Wes to my brother. That does not mean they are not excellent men."

"This is true, but I just think it is wise to consider such a thing. He must treat you well." She pulled in a deep steadying breath as quietly as she was able. There was no need to alert Georgiana to the fact that she was finding the fulfilling part of her promise frightening.

"I will insist upon it," Georgiana assured her.

"Good." Then, there was nothing to fear. Right? How did Jane stay so calm when she was called on to advise her sisters? And how did she manage to have so many good answers to questions?

"Oh, I am excited for you," Georgiana whispered as they entered the drawing room where callers were received. "Mr. Langley! You are early, are you not?"

There standing in front of the yellow settee near the window, upon which he had been seated, was Mr. Alfred Langley.

"My cousin was anxious to call on Mr. Darcy before he took Miss Bennet for a drive, so here I am waiting for you and Mrs. Darcy. I do hope our early arrival is not an inconvenience."

Lorcan was speaking to Mr. Darcy? Oh, that was wonderful news. He obviously had not changed his mind about offering for her. Her heart settled somewhat, and the fluttering in her stomach softened.

"Has your time in town been pleasant?" Kitty took a seat in a chair next to the settee while Georgiana took the place next to Mr. Alfred Langley.

"It has been."

"I have heard that you may have found success in finding a living," she continued.

Normally, Kitty was good at making conversation with gentleman callers, but her mind was not usually divided between entertaining one gentleman while wondering what was being said between the gentleman she loved and her guardian.

Yesterday, before she had left Netherfield, Papa had told Mr. Darcy, in front of her, that he trusted Mr. Darcy's opinion completely when it came to approving of a courtship or even a betrothal if there should be a gentleman who might be snared by her, either while she was in town or at Pemberley. Mama had demanded a letter be sent immediately if such a thing should happen, and Mr. Darcy had assured her that he would see her last daughter safely matched and excessively happy. She loved how Mr. Darcy frequently showed his care for her mother and father as if they were his own parents, which she supposed they really were now that he and Lizzy were married.

"Kitty," Georgiana said softly.

"Oh!" Kitty's cheeks burned. "Do forgive me. I truly was interested in hearing about your success, but –"

"There is no need to apologize, Miss Bennet," Alfred assured her. "It is an eventful day for you, and therefore, it is perfectly understandable that your attention might be elsewhere."

His smile was kind, and he did not appear to be

laughing at her, nor did he tease, even if his eyes did hold amusement. Yes, he would be a good place for her friend to begin her study of gentlemen.

"If you were to repeat what you have said, I will do my best to attend to what you are saying."

"May I, rather, ask you something before I do?"

"Yes, of course."

"It is about my cousin." He held her gaze for a moment without speaking and then said, "I know I am a torment to Lori, but I care for him very much as one would a brother. He is actually just a bit younger than my brother John." Again, he paused and just looked at her before continuing. "Do you love him? I know that is a very direct thing to ask and extremely personal when we are only just acquainted. However, I know my aunt and mother will both require an answer from me about the lady whom Lori has chosen."

"Your family is very close then?" Georgiana asked, and Kitty was happy to have Mr. Alfred Langley's attention diverted for a moment.

"Yes, very. Much like you and your brother are close to Lord and Lady Matlock." He turned back to Kitty.

"I love him most dearly," Kitty replied. "Nearly from when I first met him."

Alfred's eyebrows rose over inquisitive eyes.

"I did not refuse him because I do not love him." She willed her eyes to stay looking into Alfred's instead of dropping to study her hands as they wished to do.

"She refused on my account," Georgiana whispered.

"Georgie," Kitty protested in shock.

"I do not mind if he knows," Georgiana replied before turning back to Alfred. "She had promised to stand by my side during my first season, and she would not put her desires above remaining true to her word. But please, do not tell anyone that."

Alfred relaxed into the settee a bit further and smiled. "I would not dream of divulging such a secret." Then, shifting his eyes to Kitty he said, "I commend you on your loyalty to your friend."

"And sister," Kitty added. "We are sisters now."

"Indeed, you are."

"I have been fortunate to go from having no sisters to five in the space of a half-hour at a church. Not everyone comes by so many sisters so easily," Georgiana said.

Alfred chuckled. "That is very true. I take this to mean that neither of you views marriage as only joining yourself to a particular gentleman but that you see it also as gaining another family?"

"It goes without saying that a gentleman did not arrive in this world alone. He must have some relations. Of course, he may have outlived all of them, but they are still part of who he is," Georgiana replied. "I know I would not wish to be parted from my brother by any gentleman who marries me. I think it is only right that I extend the same courtesy."

"Wisely said, Miss Darcy," Alfred commended.

Kitty knew that her friend's wisdom had been hard gained and costly. She had been saved both from ruin and, most likely, being lost to her brother, or nearly so, by the serendipitous arrival of that brother in Ramsgate. She had seen the ugly side of how some gentlemen treat marriage as nothing more than a means of increasing their wealth. This was why she was so nervous about her season. She was an heiress and the niece of an earl. There would be many who would pretend to love her when, in reality, they were only truly in love with her money.

"Kitty," Elizabeth said as she entered the room with Mr. Darcy, "there is a gentleman who would like to speak with you in my husband's study." She was smiling broadly.

Kitty shifted her eyes to Mr. Darcy, who was also looking pleased. "I have your permission?"

He nodded and stepped into the hall with her. "Your father would be delighted, but only if this is what you desire."

"It is. It truly is."

"Then, go speak with Mr. Langley."

"Thank you," Kitty said before hurrying down the corridor to where Lorcan waited for her.

He was waiting for her! What a marvelous thought!

She could see him through the partially open door as she approached Mr. Darcy's study. Oh, how had she been granted such a wonderful second chance? She surely was the most fortunate creature to have ever lived.

"You wished to speak with me?"

Lorcan was standing just inside the door watching for her, and when she had entered, he took her hands in his eagerly. "Yes. I have been waiting to speak to you since we parted at Netherfield, and I should likely make some pleasantries and ask you if you are well and how your journey was. However, I find I do not have the patience for such things. I can see that you are well, and I will assume since you do not appear to have any injuries that your journey was good."

"It was, and I am," Kitty said with a giggle.

"Tell me, for I am most anxious to discover my fate, have you considered your promise and come to a conclusion?" He led her to the chairs by the hearth.

She sat in one, and he took the footstool in front of her so that he could still hold her hands.

"I have. Would you like to know what my promise is? I am at liberty to tell you."

He shook his head. "I do not need to know. I thought that I did, but I do not."

She pulled a hand free from his grasp and, leaning forward, placed it on his cheek. "Oh, but you do need to know, for I have promised I would tell you about it."

He turned his head and kissed her palm. "Then, tell me about it, but not until after I have asked you this." He slid off the stool on which he sat and knelt before her. "I do need to know what your promise is or to whom you have made it, though I suspect I know that." He paused. "There is only one thing I need, and that is for you to accept my heart and promise yours in return so that I might cherish it forever. I love you so dearly that the mere thought of being without you makes every fiber of my being ache. The month I spent believing I had lost you was a torment I wish never to endure again. Will you marry me – not now, but in the future when your duty to your friend is complete?"

The joy which had been cautiously dancing within her burst forth in a broad smile. Never in all of her imaginings as she had pressed flowers into her book in her room had she ever dreamt of a gentleman declaring his love for her in such ardent terms. Nor had she considered that one would love her enough to wait for her, though he did not even know how long that might be or why. Yet, here, kneeling before her, was such a gentleman – one whom she thought she had lost. Again, she could not believe her good fortune.

"My dearest Lorcan, yes, I will most happily marry you when my duty is done, for you already hold my heart."

Before she could say anything more to declare

her love for him, he had risen and pulled her into his embrace. "Thank you. Thank you, my dearest love," he whispered as he lowered his head and, just as had happened in the music room at Matlock House, the touch of his lips to hers ignited something within her which was so powerful that it could not be controlled. She wound her arms around his neck and pressed herself against him as if the air between them was too great a gap.

Desire thrummed through her as one of his hands pressed against her back and held her firmly while the other hand cradled the back of her head. However, it was not her desire alone that made this feeling of being held and kissed by him so powerful. It was the mingling of that desire with a wonderful knowledge that rose from her heart and spread through her. It was the same knowledge which had only whispered of love and happiness on that fateful day in the music room. However, now, as she tangled her fingers in her beloved's hair and he sighed with pleasure, it shouted not only of love and happiness but also about being cherished and having found her one true and lasting love.

Before You Go

If you enjoyed this book, be sure to let others
know by leaving a review.

~*~*~

Want to know when other books in this series
will be available?
You can always know what's new with my
books by subscribing to my mailing list.
(There will, of course, be a thank you gift for
joining because I think my readers are awesome!)
Book News from Leenie Brown
(bit.ly/LeenieBBookNews)

~*~*~

Turn the page to read an excerpt of another one
of Leenie's books

His Inconvenient
Choice Excerpt

*If you like Pride and Prejudice variation series such as
the Marrying Elizabeth series, I have written a couple
of others including the Choices series. Below is an
excerpt from His Inconvenient Choice, which is book 3
in that series and stars Kitty Bennet as the heroine.*

CHAPTER 1

January 1, 1812

Colonel Richard Fitzwilliam unfolded the small
piece of paper that had been tucked into his pocket
as he left Netherfield after the wedding breakfast.
He shook his head. Two cousins and a friend married all within the space of two weeks was enough
to set anyone's world on end. It was also the sort of
thing that made him contemplate his own future.
Such thoughts often made his breathing feel

forced. He drew a deep breath, trying to rid his body of the feeling of being crushed, but it was only slightly helpful. He knew that his future was not to be so happy as those of his cousins and Bingley. He was not free to choose where he wished. His marriage would be one of convenience; his father would see to that.

He looked surreptitiously at the paper in his palm, not wishing to draw attention to it from the others in the carriage. The drawing there brought a smile to his lips and a pang of regret to his heart. Forget-me-nots graced the lid of a box from which spilled strands of pearls and chains of gold. He folded the drawing again and slipped it back into his pocket. If his heart could make his choice for him instead of his father, Kitty Bennet would be his choice. She had stolen his heart when she shivered in the wind on the street in front of the milliner's shop as she insisted on being introduced to him as Katherine. Upon further acquaintance, she had proven to be a lady who shared many of his same interests and who made him feel at ease. She expected no more from him than to be himself. He did not need to be a military leader or the son of an earl. She was interested in his wooden creations — and not as a lady who was trying to make a favourable impression on a gentleman. No, she listened with interest and animation. She had even sketched a few designs that he might like to use.

"If you could wait but a year," she had said as they strolled the perimeter of the ballroom last evening, "then your inheritance would be yours."

"He will not allow me to be free. He will insist on my marrying before he gives me one farthing more than I have," he had replied. Her eyes had filled with tears that she refused to shed, and his heart had broken a bit more at the thought of a life without her. "If I could wait," he had whispered, "I would wait a thousand years for you."

She had smiled sadly at him and said, "And I would wait for you."

He ran his gloved finger over the drawing in the pocket of his coat. "Do not forget me," she had said as she had slipped it into his pocket when he was taking his leave of her. He knew he would never forget her. His hand closed around the paper.

"You are looking rather pensive, Colonel," said Caroline Bingley. "Are they pleasant thoughts?"

"Not all of them," he said as he turned to look

out the window. If the weather had not been so foul, he would have refused Hurst's offer to travel with him.

"That is a pity," said Louisa. "I prefer to think on pleasant things whenever possible."

"As do I," said Richard, "but it is not always possible."

"A colonel must have many unpleasant things to consider," added Caroline.

"He must," said Richard. "However, I was not thinking as a colonel but as a mere man."

Hurst snorted at the comment. "Do leave him be, Caroline."

"I was only attempting to pass the time in conversation," she replied with a huff. "The light is too poor for anything else."

"I find a quiet nap a most refreshing way to pass a trip," replied Hurst.

"How dull," said Caroline.

"Not at all," said Richard. "I find I would like to close my eyes. It has been a busy two days."

Hurst nodded. "You were out with your men yesterday, were you not?"

"I put them through a few drills to test them. Those who passed were allowed to attend the ball.

Those who did not pass were confined to quarters for the evening." It had been his plan, and a successful one, to keep Wickham from the ball. He would take every opportunity afforded him by his position to ensure that Wickham had less pleasure than he desired. It was the one pleasure he received from his duty.

"And, I believe, you danced every dance, did you not?" asked Louisa.

"All save one." His heart pinched, for that one had been set aside to stroll with Kitty.

"Oh, Hurst, you are right. I do believe a nap must be had. What with an early morning yesterday for the colonel, a night of dancing, and another early start to the day today, he must be very tired." She turned to Caroline. "It would be unkind of us to keep him from his rest."

"I thank you," said Richard with a bow of his head. Then added, "I am indeed rather tired," as he settled back and closed his eyes.

Conversation with anyone at present would be unpleasant; with Caroline Bingley, it would be even more so. His fingers once again sought that slip of paper in his pocket. Finding it, he allowed his mind to wander to the lady who had given it to him, and with a deep exhale, he attempted to find some peace in sleep.

~*~*~*~*~*~

"Mr. Darcy, might I have a word with you?" Kitty turned from the window where she had been watching the Hursts' carriage drive away. There were not many wedding guests remaining, and she knew that both she and the Darcys would leave soon.

"Certainly," replied Darcy. He had not had very many opportunities to speak with Kitty. She seemed to avoid him whenever possible, and so her request surprised him. He watched her twist her fingers together and bite her lip, signs that he had learned through watching his wife indicated she was nervous.

"I have a little bit of money and expect to receive some more." She resisted the urge to duck her head and hide from him. His presence had always unsettled her. She was sure he was at any moment going to scold her for some foolishness. She knew she had no reason to feel so, but she did. However, she also knew that he would best be able to advise her, and so she straightened her shoulders and continued. "I have sold some designs to Mrs. Havelston, and she has requested some more. I have not signed them with my name, and it is to be a secret arrangement." The words rushed from her. "I would like to invest it. I know that you can earn money with money, but I do not know how to do it, and I am not a gentleman, which limits me."

He smiled at her. "That sounds like a wise thing to do."

Her brows drew together. "It does?"

"Indeed." He smiled at her again and was rewarded with a small smile in return.

She withdrew a small velvet pouch from her reticule. "It is really very little. It may not be enough to invest yet, but I dare not place it in my father's strongbox, for if something happens to him, I do not wish to explain it to Mr. Collins."

Darcy took the bag from her and slipped it into his pocket. "I shall care for it. You will keep a record of what you have given me, and I will do the same. You know how to do this?"

She pursed her lips and drew her brows together. "I will have my father show me."

"Very good."

"Mr. Darcy, could we save some time and trouble if I request my uncle to give the money to you?"

She twisted her hands again. "He regularly receives payments from Mrs. Havelston for her orders, so no one would suspect she is paying me if she gives it to him. And if he meets with you, no one would question the activity."

He nodded. The thought she had put into her plans impressed him. If he were perfectly honest with himself, he would not have thought her capable of such well-thought out plans. She had, on the occasions when he had been in her company before his marriage to Elizabeth, struck him as flighty and silly. He chided himself. He had not noted such behaviour since their arrival last week. "I understand. This is an arrangement that is to be private."

"Very. If anyone was to learn that I was earning money…"

"I understand," said Darcy. "Do you have a plan in mind for the money?"

The tears that had been threatening all morning sprang to her eyes, and her cheeks flushed in embarrassment.

"You do not have to tell me," Darcy said quietly.

She shook her head. "I have a foolish notion that will probably be unsuccessful, but your cousin should not be forced to give up what he loves. I thought perhaps I could help him find a way to be happy." She shrugged. "If not, then the money can be added to my portion, which will be of assistance to me when I need to set up my own establishment. I do not wish to live solely on the charity of my relations."

"You do not plan to marry?" Darcy asked in some surprise.

The tears once again gathered in her eyes, and she blinked against them as she shook her head. "I had hoped," she said softly.

His eyes followed her gaze toward the window and the drive at Netherfield. "One must not lose hope, Miss Kitty. Circumstances can change."

She drew a deep breath and released it slowly as she steadied her emotions. Then, she gave him as much of smile as she could manage. "While I own that it is not an utter impossibility, I think it highly unlikely."

He nodded as she thanked him and went to join her father, who was saying his farewells to Elizabeth and Jane. Elizabeth caught Darcy's eye and gave him a questioning look and in response, he shrugged and smiled.

"You look troubled, my dear," she said as she slipped her arm into his and waved to her father's carriage.

"I believe I am," he said as he assisted her into their carriage. Then, he gave one more wave to Bingley and climbed in beside her. Shaking the rain from his hat, he set it on the bench across from them before tucking a blanket across their laps. "Shall we pass the journey as we did on our wedding day?"

She giggled. "I should like that very much, Mr. Darcy, but not until you tell me what has you troubled. I shall not be distracted by your sweet kisses until I know all."

"Is that a fact?" He leaned over and kissed her softly.

She smiled and pushed at his chest. "I would like nothing better than to be distracted so pleasantly, sir, but I am afraid my mind will not be settled until you have told me about what you and Kitty were speaking."

He gave her a quick kiss before she could stop him. "Very well. Your sister has asked me to help her with her finances. It seems she has sold some designs and intends to sell some more, and she wishes to have her earnings invested."

"And this has you troubled?" Elizabeth's brows furrowed as one eyebrow rose in disbelief. "Is it that she is earning money which has concerned you?"

He chuckled and shook his head. "Her selling designs and wishing to invest is not what has me troubled. I asked her what she intended to do with the money, and she nearly cried." He stroked Elizabeth's cheek with his thumb and smiled sadly at her. "Based on her answers and my cousin's strange behaviour last night and this morning, I believe she has had her heart broken by my uncle." He first gave Elizabeth's pursed lips a kiss and then the deep furrow between her brows. "She wishes to help Richard with her money. She does not wish to see him forced to give up what he loves. She also said she no longer intends to marry." He wrapped his arms around Elizabeth and drew her closer as he saw sadness enter her eyes. "And that has me troubled, for I do not wish to see either her or Richard give up whom they love."

"What can be done?" Elizabeth peeked up at him from where her head rested on his shoulder.

"I do not know. My uncle will make it challenging. He wishes a marriage of advantage for Richard, one that will strengthen his political ties and increase Richard's wealth. It will take some thought. However, nothing can be done at present." He kissed her forehead again. "And now, Mrs. Darcy, since I have told you all that is troubling me, I believe I may now distract you with kisses."

She wrapped her arms around his neck. "I believe you must." And eagerly, he obliged.

~*~*~*~*~*~

Richard handed his hat and coat to Harrison, the Matlocks' butler, and slipped into his mother's sitting room to greet her.

Lady Matlock held him close for a moment. "I am happy to see you safely returned to me. Will you be staying?" She took a seat on a settee and motioned for him to join her.

"I have no choice. I do not wish to impose on Darcy or Rycroft as they are settling in with their wives."

"There is BayLeafe," his mother said softly. BayLeafe was the small estate just outside of town which was part of the inheritance that should come to him through his mother should his father see fit to give it him.

He shook his head at her offering.

"Your father is in quite a state what with both of your cousins marrying outside of what is proper." She reached up and brushed his hair back from his forehead. "He is not all bad, you know. He has been good to me. He is just set in his ways."

"Do you love him?" Richard's voice was soft.

"I suppose I do," she replied. "It is possible to become friends and then more even when you begin as near strangers." She took his hand. "I cannot say I have never wished for more or for another, for I did at first, but now, I cannot imagine my life in any other way."

Richard nodded and placed the small folded drawing in her hand. "You would have liked her," he said as she unfolded the paper. Where his father blustered, his mother spoke softly. Where his father was arrogant, she demonstrated grace and humility. They were in many ways as opposed as darkness and light.

She lay the drawing on her lap, a hand resting on her heart. "It is very well done. Who is she?"

He shook his head and took the paper from her

lap. "It matters not, for it shall never be." He rose and went to the window. "She has neither wealth nor significant connections beyond our family."

Lady Matlock came to stand near him. "She is connected to our family?"

He nodded. "Her sisters are the new Mrs. Darcy and Lady Rycroft." He turned toward her. "And that is not the worst of it. A third sister is the new Mrs. Bingley." He watched her struggle with how to accept this information. He knew she loved him and would wish him only to be happy, but she also held to some of the same ideas regarding marriage as her husband. It was not only his father who wished him to make a good match. He tucked the paper in his pocket. "As I said, it matters not, for it shall never be. My heart is of little importance."

Raised voices could be heard from somewhere down the hall.

"Your aunt Catherine is here," his mother said in answer to his questioning look. "Anne is with her but has taken to her room, whether it is due to ill health or a need to avoid her mother, I am uncertain."

Just then, Lady Catherine stomped into the sitting room. "He is as unreasonable as ever!"

"I am not being unreasonable. You are being daft. To accept such connections into the family without some censure? And after he did not marry Anne as we had planned?" Lord Matlock threw his hands up as if unable to fathom the thoughts.

"It would be better for Anne to marry someone with higher connections," said Lady Catherine, "a peer or the son of a peer." Her eyes came to rest on Richard. "Even a second son would do."

A sly smile spread slowly across Lord Matlock's face. "That is an idea. It would keep all the land holding within the family." He clapped his hands together and rubbed them back and forth. "I shall have my solicitor draw up the arrangement. Shall we have the wedding in two months? I do think that would give enough time to find him a replacement with his unit and ready the necessary items for the release of his inheritance, but I will have to defer to my solicitor and man of business for advice before we finalize the date." He leveled a hard glare at Richard. "Any objection shall be met with a significant, if not permanent breach. Do I make myself clear?"

Richard shook his head in disbelief. "I am no more to you than that?"

"On the contrary," said his father, "you are of great significance, and that is why your future must be secured. Were something to ever happen to your brother, you would need to secure the title with an appropriate heir, one with an acceptable lineage."

Richard's jaw clenched. "So I am a well-bred horse in your stable then, whose only expectation is to sire the next prize stallion. And if I do not, I, like that horse, shall be turned out to work alongside the other workhorses on the estate."

His father's eyes narrowed. "Not on my estates." His voice held more than a little warning.

Richard stepped closer and pulled himself up to his full height, which was two inches taller than his father. "And if you turn me out and something happens to my brother, then where will your precious title fall? Ah, yes, to your brother." The comment caused the reaction he desired. His father took a step back and his face paled slightly. "Two weeks," Richard said. "I ask two weeks to consider your offer, sir."

"What is there to consider?" said Lady Catherine.

"The value of my life," Richard snarled. He

moved toward the door, but his mother's hand on his arm forestalled him.

"I will see you again?" Her eyes were filled with fear.

"At least once more," he murmured as he kissed her cheek before leaving the room and instructing that his things be readied for a journey.

Acknowledgments

There are many who have had a part in the creation of this story. Some have read and commented on it. Some have proofread for grammatical errors and plot holes. Others have not even read the story and a few, I know, will never read it. However, their encouragement and belief in my ability, as well as their patience when I became cranky or when supper was late or the groceries ran low, was invaluable.

And so, I would like to say *thank you* to Zoe, Rose, Kristine, Ben, and Kyle, as well as my patrons on Patreon and the readers who faithfully read all those Thursday posts on my blog. I feel blessed by your help, support, and understanding.

I have not listed my dear husband in the above group because, to me, he deserves his own special thank you, for, without his somewhat pushy insistence that I start sharing my writing, none of my writing goals and dreams would have been met.

For those who might be interested in some of the visual inspiration I used while writing this book — I have a Pinterest board for that.

Other Leenie B Books

You can find all of Leenie's books at this link
bit.ly/LeenieBBooks
where you can explore the collections below

~*~

Other Pens, Mansfield Park

~*~

Touches of Austen Collection

~*~

Dash of Darcy and Companions Collection

~*~

Marrying Elizabeth Series

~*~

Willow Hall Romances

~*~

The Choices Series

~*~

Darcy Family Holidays

~*~

Darcy and... An Austen-Inspired Collection

~*~

Nature's Fury and Delights (A Sweet Regency Novelettes Series)

About the Author

Leenie Brown has always been a girl with an active imagination, which, while growing up, was both an asset, providing many hours of fun as she played out stories, and a liability, when her older sister and aunt would tell her frightening tales. At one time, they had her convinced Dracula lived in the trunk at the end of the bed she slept in when visiting her grandparents!

Although it has been years since she cowered in her bed in her grandparents' basement, she still has an imagination which occasionally runs away with her, and she feeds it now as she did then — by reading!

Her heroes, when growing up, were authors, and the worlds they painted with words were (and still are) her favourite playgrounds! Now, as an adult, she spends much of her time in the Regency world, playing with the characters from her favourite Jane Austen novels and those of her own creation.

When she is not traipsing down a trail in an attempt to keep up with her imagination, Leenie resides in the beautiful province of Nova Scotia with her two sons and her very own Mr. Brown (a wonderful mix of all the best of Darcy, Bingley, and Edmund with a healthy dose of the teasing Mr. Tilney and just a dash of the scolding Mr. Knightley).

Connect with Leenie

E-mail:
LeenieBrownAuthor@gmail.com
Facebook:
www.facebook.com/LeenieBrownAuthor
Blog:
leeniebrown.com
Patreon:
https://www.patreon.com/LeenieBrown
Subscribe to Leenie's Mailing List:
Book News from Leenie Brown
(bit.ly/LeenieBBookNews)